SHAMEFULLY SHARED

LOKI RENARD

CHAPTER ONE

Chase

"You have *got* to be fucking kidding me. No. No way! Are you crazy? We're not helping *her*!"

Chase Rathkeale stood calmly as Col, his best friend and an integral part of their unit swore up a storm. He was all dressed up and ready to go in black fatigues, his dark hair cropped close to his head, his handsome features twisted with disbelief and outrage. All had been fine until Chase had made the tactical error of telling him where they were going and why. He should have waited until they were on the freeway to say anything.

"She needs us."

"No. Absolutely not. I'm not lifting a finger to save her after what she did."

"Rex, Max, and Brian are all waiting in the van," Chase said. "We need you, buddy. Do it for us, not for her."

Col rounded on him, finger pointed. "You always wanted to fuck her. You should have done it back then. Got it out of your system."

"This isn't about sex, Col."

"What is it about, then?"

"It's about a woman who needs our help."

"Oh. A woman needs our help," Col sneered. "And this one, unlike the tens of thousands of other women who need help in this country, just happens to also have seriously fucked us over. Hard. Is she paying us?"

"Well…"

"No, of course she fucking isn't." Col let out a dark laugh and threw his hands up. "What is it with her? Why is she the damsel that just has to be rescued? She fucking betrayed us, Chase. She ruined our lives. And you expect me to help her?"

"I expect you to follow orders."

The voice that spoke wasn't Chase's. It belonged to Rex. At thirty-eight years of age, he was the senior member of their group. His dark hair was flecked with gray toward his temples and he carried a gravitas that made him seem far older than his years sometimes. Before they'd been dishonorably discharged, he had been their captain. Now he was the boss.

Col shut his mouth, gritting his teeth.

"You don't need to worry if she's paying us, because I'm paying you," Rex continued. "And I expect you to do your job without complaint. We're moving out. Now."

Chase waited to see what would happen. There were only five of them in their elite private security unit. That was what they called it anyway. The rest of the world had a different name for them: mercenaries. Of the five, Col was usually the least likely to disobey a direct order. He had been the golden boy before the incident that had seen their likenesses splashed across every newspaper and website in the country, and before the military had cut them loose as national embarrassments.

"Rex…" Col's voice dropped to a near whine. "Why? Just tell me why?"

"Have I ever told you why?" Rex fixed Col with a steely look. "I've told you to do a thousand things far more dangerous than this, and now you decide to start questioning my judgment?"

Rex was pulling rank. It was a risky move given how pissed off Col was. There was every chance Col would finally snap and tell Rex and the rest of them to go fuck themselves. He'd been close a few times before, but never this close.

It worked.

Col swore under his breath and picked up the pack he'd already prepared. "Alright," he said. "Let's go."

Chase followed Col out to the van, taking up the rear as they piled in. Brian had the wheel. He was the smartest guy Chase had ever met, bar absolutely none. Genius-level intellect and a twisted personality to match. Chase didn't know how Brian felt about the mission. Actually, Chase wasn't sure he had feelings at all. Everything was a problem to be analyzed for Brian. He was less well built than the rest of them, but he was still well over six foot and twice as powerful as most men.

As Chase got in, he noticed that the only guy who looked happy about this was Max. Max was hanging out the window, banging on the side of the van. He'd taken the opportunity of leaving the military to grow his dirty blond hair out to the base of his neck and he usually sported a five or even ten o'clock shadow. Right now he had sunglasses pushed up over his head and was doing his best impression of a 1980s action hero.

"So we're really doing this," Col said, taking the center seat. "We're going to help Lacey Christie. This is some serious…" He trailed off as Rex sat next to him. The cursing that would have escaped him was cut off abruptly. Rex quite often positioned himself next to Col, like a physical fuse on his temper.

"Don't worry," Max said from the front seat. "There's something *sweet* in it for us."

CHAPTER TWO

Lacey

Lacey bit her fingernails and twitched the blinds for the fiftieth time. She was nervous, a sheen of sweat covering her body as she paced the floor of the cheap motel room where she was holed up. She did not look her best, which shouldn't have mattered, but somehow it did. With her entire life out of control, at least looking somewhat put together would have made her feel a little better.

She was wearing gym clothes. Dark leggings, a pink tank top, and near enough matching tennis shoes. Her long brown hair was drawn back off her face and tied in a ponytail. In preparation for seeing Chase again, she'd tried to enhance her appearance with a bit of mascara and the remains of a tube of lipstick she'd found in her glovebox. She had nothing else. Her apartment was too dangerous to go back to. She'd been on her way to the gym when she'd realized she'd forgotten her ionized water and headed home just in time to see two shadowy figures through the window.

Most people would have interpreted that as a sign of a burglary in progress and called the police, but Lacey knew better. She knew three other journalists, her closest friends and professional confidantes, were dead. She knew that all their deaths had occurred in their homes, a series of unfortunate 'accidents' that weren't accidents at all. She had footage from the last one, and in that she had seen those shadowy figures moving around before they got her friend. She was not going to stick around to find out how she was supposed to go out. So far it had been slipping in the shower, accidental electrocution by faulty blender, and a home gym weightlifting accident.

If it weren't for Adam getting suspicious and setting up a hidden camera that streamed his murder, there would be no evidence at all. But this wasn't the sort of evidence she could take to the police. This was the sort of evidence that would lead to her dying in a cell. The people she had crossed were not ones to be concerned by police. They owned the police. And they wanted to own the media too.

With nowhere left to turn to, she'd fled to a shitty motel on the outskirts of Washington DC, knowing there was only one person she could call. Unfortunately, he didn't owe her a favor. He didn't owe her a damn thing. She owed him everything.

To her utter shock, once she'd given him a hurried explanation of what was happening, he'd agreed to come. Right away. That she hadn't expected. He wasn't as far away as she'd thought either. They were all based in Washington, apparently, though she was now looking to get as far away as possible, as quickly as possible.

A big dark van pulled up outside her room. She held her breath as someone got out of the driver's side. Tall, dark hair, handsome, maybe mid-twenties. She didn't recognize him, but he did look familiar somehow. He wasn't Chase. Another guy got out of the other side, shaggy blond hair down to his collar, sexy in spite of some facial scarring. Him, she did recognize. That was Max Brolin. The back of the van opened and three more men got out.

Had Chase brought… everybody?

She took a step back from the blinds and tried to gather

herself and her thoughts. Everybody. All of them. This was the reunion she'd hoped would never happen.

A heavy knock at the door startled her, even though she knew exactly who it was. She hesitated, not knowing if she should open it. These weren't friends, in any sense of the word. Chase alone was a risk. The whole clan?

It had been three years since she last saw them. Two and a half since she'd ruined their lives. God. This wasn't a rescue mission. This was... she glanced toward the back of the motel unit, wondered if she could make it out the back.

Another hard knock brought her out of her panic and made her think a little more rationally. There was no running away from these guys. Maybe Chase had just brought them as backup. Now wasn't the time to be refusing help, no matter where it came from.

Lacey opened the door and saw Chase standing there, looking down at her from his great height. She was 5'4, a respectable height for a woman. He was a giant of a man, 6'3 and counting. She gazed up at him, her heart skipping a beat as she was instantly transported to the first time she'd ever looked into those stunning blue and gold eyes.

• • • • • • •

Three years earlier

Lacey tried to get comfortable on a hard stone ledge that doubled as her bed. She was barely able to move thanks to the ropes that were biting into her skin, causing sores that were already getting weepy in the Venezuelan heat. The little room stank. There was an uncovered bucket half-full of her own waste in the corner, which made things even worse. It was hot and dark and oppressive in that little cell, which was barely the size of a single closet. There were no windows. There was no fresh air and the light came from a single incandescent bulb that burned continuously. Flies swarmed around the bucket in an ever present cloud that was the only way she could tell the time. They slept in the evening and rose in the morning, their little insect brains attuned to the world she was no longer part of.

"American spy bitch!"

The guard's vicious voice made her tremble as he came past and banged on the iron door. Every time they came to see her they threatened to kill her. She was sure that they would make good on that threat sooner or later. Probably sooner. She wasn't a spy, but she knew she'd seen too much for them to let her live. What truly frightened her was the reason they were keeping her alive. What were they going to do with her? Ransom her, maybe. That was about the best case scenario. All of the others she could think of were far worse.

She didn't know anything, but that didn't stop them from dragging her out every few hours or days and screaming questions at her. Press credentials hadn't satisfied them that she wasn't a spy. They refused to contact her editor to confirm her identity. Apparently he was a spy as well. Everyone and everything was a spy to these paranoid militia who were trafficking so much cocaine they basically bathed in the stuff. There wasn't one of them that didn't have perpetually dilated pupils, a powder mustache, and a nasty teeth-grinding habit that made them grimace from time to time, their sweaty cruel faces contorting in demonic ways that made her sick to her stomach with fear.

Half the questions they asked didn't make any sense. The other half were so far out of her realm of knowledge that she could barely think of anything to stutter in response. At first it had been terrifying, but as the days had gone on, her body had adapted into a survival mode and she was no longer fully aware of her own fear, except in the moments between the bolts of pure terror that were evoked every time one of her guards came near.

Tense, she waited for the guard to come back. She was hungry and thirsty. Sometimes they refused to let her eat or drink until she told them something. She'd told them everything they wanted to hear. She'd told them lie after lie. She'd told them the truth too. None of it mattered because it didn't really matter what she said.

Loud bangs outside made her cringe. Her captive mind was unable to parse the sensory information with any kind of hope. It sounded like gunfire. Were they practicing for her? Were they fighting each other? Were they just discharging weapons at random? Anything was possible. Paranoia was everywhere, and had sunk into her bones. She couldn't help but hear her death in the sounds that were growing closer.

Lacey began to whisper the only prayer she knew under her breath. These weeks in Venezuela had taught her there was no God, but she prayed anyway, because it was all she had.

Bam!

The door burst open, a gun was pointed straight at her face, and her eyes widened as she saw the most beautiful thing she had ever seen in her life: an American soldier. He was dressed from head to toe in black tactical gear without any kind of identifying markings. His face was covered aside from his eyes, two brilliant blue orbs the color of the sky. There was no real sign that he was what she thought he was, but she knew in the core of her being that he was American. She knew. She just fucking knew.

She started screaming. "Help me! I'm a journalist! They've captured me!"

He stared at her, his weapon lowered to the floor. For a second, absolutely nothing happened. Then he spoke.

"Shit."

That was the first word she'd ever heard Chase Rathkeale say. A curse word in a mid-West accent. It was like hearing a choir of angels sing and she burst into tears of pure relief.

· · · · · · ·

She could burst into tears right now, just seeing him again. It took a real effort not to throw herself into his arms, but she resisted, not knowing the kind of reception that would get. He'd come, but that didn't mean he'd forgiven her.

"Hi," she said, hoping she didn't sound as shy as she felt. "Come in, please."

She held the door open as the men filed in. She looked at their hard faces carefully, trying to work out where sympathy lay. Chase, sickeningly handsome, was the only one to really make eye contact with her. The others either stared over her head or through her completely. The one at the end wouldn't look at her at all. His jaw was twitching as he stared at the shitty motel art.

"Are you okay?" Chase looked at her with concern.

God, he was handsome.

"Um, yeah. I mean, I don't think they saw me. I think they're still waiting for me to get home. I don't know."

"Okay," he said, taking her by the arms. He moved her around and sat her on the end of the bed, which left her looking up at the line of men and then he crouched down in front of her, holding her attention with his gaze. "Tell me what happened."

"I went home and…" She launched into a description of the events of the day, and those that had come before it. Pulling out her cellphone, she showed him, and by proxy, the rest of the silent men, precisely why she was so sure that death was stalking her. It was the footage Adam had taken. The evidence that proved his death was no accident whatsoever.

"His name was Adam Stern," she said. "He'd been followed and he thought something might happen so he set up cameras in his apartment that streamed to our secure server."

Tinny voices were raised through her phone's speakers. She heard Adam's last words. They weren't brave. They were confused and laced with fear. Lacey knew what

9

happened next. She half-shut her eyes, but she could still hear the sickening sound of a heavy bar of weights being dropped on his prone neck.

Chase didn't so much as wince. He took the phone from her limp fingers, and she let him have it.

"So you've got this," he said, no reaction whatsoever to seeing a man die. "Anything else?"

"I've got a lot of stuff," she said. "We worked independently to uncover a range of crimes. They all led back to Senator Fishland. You know, the one with those shitty ads where he's fishing and then he makes that dumb joke about being a fish out of water? That guy has fingers in every fucked-up pie there is. There's not a criminal syndicate in the country that doesn't own him. He has ties into the FBI for sure, likely the CIA as well. He's pretty much untouchable at this point. I guess that's why he got so blatant with some of it. Anyway, everyone had a piece of the puzzle, and everything was encrypted. That was supposed to keep us safe. There's a system. We were all linked up to it, and when any of us didn't sign on for a twenty-four-hour period, the information we held was sent to those who still had active accounts. I have the last one. I have everything. And it's, uhm… it's a lot."

Chase nodded and stood up, turning to the others. "See?"

She didn't understand the significance of the word, but obviously he'd just proved something to his men.

"I'm really surprised you all came," she said. "I didn't expect, I mean, I know… I'm so sorry about what happened. I had no idea you'd be… I had no idea… I thought you'd be heroes. You were heroes to me."

She hoped that her little speech would soften them, but it didn't seem to help. Five sets of distinctly unimpressed eyes settled on her with hard expressions. A couple of sweet words weren't going to make things better. Lacey understood that. What she didn't understand was why they were all there.

"Uhm, I really don't expect you all to help me," she said. "I don't expect any of you to. I just called Chase because I needed to know how to survive this…"

"Well, you won't survive it alone," Chase said decisively. "You're dealing with shadow government agents. They have abilities and powers no other organization does. How did you check in here?"

"Cash," she said. "I'm not dumb enough to use my credit card for anything."

"Is that your car out front?"

Her little yellow Kia Forte was parked next to their big black behemoth.

"Yeah."

"They won't be far off," the tall dark-haired one with the innocent face said. "We passed a bunch of plate readers on the way here."

Suddenly nervous, Lacey popped up from the bed. Chase reached out with one hand and pushed her back down into a sitting position.

"Easy, Ms. Christie," he said. "The pattern of deaths is concerning. It sounds like you and your friends really were on to something."

"We were," she said. "I'm going to take it to mass media. That's the only way to spread it. The story can't be buried…"

"Easy," Chase soothed. "You're already in over your head. Let's not make that worse."

She bristled, wanting to deny that, but she couldn't. She'd been in over her head when they first met, and she was drowning now.

"So. Uhm… I appreciate this, but I mean… how…" She just had to ask the question outright. "How can you help me?"

"Since we got booted from the service, we started our own little mercenary unit. We're pretty well equipped, Lacey."

"Wow," she said. "I called the right guys then. You

landed on your feet. That's awesome. I'm so happy for you."

She smiled around at them all. There was not a single smile back. What on earth was going on? They were there, but they didn't seem happy—and she got that, but if they didn't want to help her, then why had they come?"

An uncomfortable feeling started to build in her belly. The relief and nervousness that had overwhelmed her when she first saw them was starting to turn. Something wasn't right. These men didn't look helpful. She suddenly felt like a lamb surrounded by a pack of wolves.

"Okay, what's going on?"

Chase glanced over at the man who had been conspicuously quiet so far. Chase hadn't been the leader of the unit when she met him in Venezuela. That role had been played by Rex Waltham. And Rex was standing more or less behind him, just off to the left, his large arms crossed over his broad chest. She'd not had much to do with him back then. He'd been the one barking orders, the one who coordinated everything. She wasn't easily intimidated, but she was nervous around him. There was just something in his steel gray gaze that sent shivers down her spine. Now that it was fixed on her, she could barely breathe.

"You want to explain, Rex?" Chase threw it over to him.

"Alright." Rex had a Texan drawl, a rough, gravelly voice that gave him natural gravitas. He was older than the other men by about a decade. Lacey was twenty-five. She'd been twenty-two when she was captured, just an idiot naive journalism grad who fancied herself an international freelancer. In the years since, she'd learned a lot about herself, and the world, but she felt small compared to him. Rex had to be in his late thirties now. The rest of them were mostly around thirty or so, except for the one on the end. He was a bit younger. The pup of the group.

Rex stepped forward, and she instinctively leaned back a little. It wasn't that he was menacing her on purpose, it was just the sheer force of his personality. Back then he'd been clean-shaven. Now there was stubble around his chin and jaw, a very closely trimmed beard of sorts. He was graying a little at the temples, but it wasn't the kind of gray that made a man look old. It was the kind that made him mature. Matched with the steel hue of his eyes, it only made him more intimidating.

"You've caused us quite a bit of trouble over the years, Miss Christie."

There was no denying that. When they'd rescued her, they'd been an elite military unit on a classified mission. They'd told her not to mention anything about their role in her rescue, but she hadn't been able to help herself. As a junior freelance journalist, the story of being rescued by elite Special Forces had been too good not to tell.

The story had been picked up and syndicated internationally. It had been her first big break, the beginning of everything—and then someone had worked out who the men in the story were, and a new scandal had developed around geopolitical relations and… basically a whole bunch of shit most people really didn't care about. The brass did though, and every single one of Rex's unit, all the men now looking at her, had been court-martialed and dishonorably discharged. That part of the story hadn't hit national news, but she'd known about it. Tried to apologize for it too, but only Chase had taken her call.

"I really didn't mean to…"

"You were told not to say anything." Rex's tone was clipped and harsh.

"I know, but…"

"There are no buts. You cost us our careers, and we were lucky that's all that you cost us. If we'd been active when that story broke, you could have cost us our lives."

"I'm sorry…"

"We're not interested in sorry," Rex said bluntly.

Her hackles were starting to rise now. Had they come just to waste her time?

"What are you interested in, then?" She was just barely keeping her temper now. From the fear she'd been filled with at seeing assassins in her apartment, to the relief when she first saw these guys again, she was now just confused, guilty, and more than a little upset.

"We understand your life is in danger," Rex said. "But you don't have the kind of money we cost, Miss Christie, and frankly, you owe us more than mere money could really cover anyway."

"So you came all this way just to tell me that you're not going to help me? Thanks," she said, bitter and sarcastic. "Hope you all have a nice drive home."

"We came to offer you a deal."

A deal? She let her eyes run over the line of hard military men. "What kind of deal?"

"We get paid to protect what belongs to other people. But we'll happily protect what's ours for free."

Her head jerked back as her gaze was drawn back to Rex again. "Uhm… what?"

"If we help you, you will belong to us. All five of us."

"Belong to… as in…"

"As in your body." Rex made things bluntly clear.

Her eyes widened in shock. He couldn't be serious. There was no way. There were *five* of them, and they expected her to… it was utterly unthinkable what they expected. This was taking advantage, pure and simple.

"You're honorable men. You can't mean this. Chase…"

"We used to be honorable. We're not so much into that these days." The one at the end bit the words out bitterly. She'd forgotten his name, but not his face. He was viciously handsome, very dark eyes that were held perpetually narrowed, dark brows, a hard jaw and lips that at the moment were a thin slash. Her heart skipped a beat. Danger. She recognized it instantly. They were all dangerous, of course, but he stood out among them, a fierce, barely restrained male force.

"There has to be something in this for us, Lacey," Chase said more reasonably. With his sandy blond hair and blue eyes, Chase looked like the boy next door—if the boy next door had been pounding protein shakes and pumping iron for the past decade. He was a good man, the only one to accept her apology for what had happened after her story broke. Her heart ached whenever she so much as looked at a picture of him, but right now she was just stunned.

"Has to be something in it for you? I thought you were better than this, Chase."

"Why? We don't really know each other, Lacey. Not like that."

Good point, she guessed. She'd known them for a couple of days in Venezuela. Same length of time they'd known her. Which was probably why they'd had the balls to make this kind of proposal. If they knew her better, they wouldn't have wasted her time and theirs.

She looked down the line of men, hoping to find some salvation. Max—she'd never forgotten that name—was grinning as if he expected her to just immediately fall in love with the idea. He'd gathered a few more scars since she'd last seen him. Had the one over the bridge of his nose always been there? *First to throw himself into action, last to care about the consequences* had been her assessment when she'd dashed out the article about them.

Then there was the last one. The younger one. Brains. No. Brian. That's right. Definition of tall, dark, and handsome. Could have been a runway model with his elongated frame. He ran the tech, from memory. She had been impressed with the alacrity with which Brian had handled a fire fight while simultaneously scrambling satellite signals and giving them a clear window for escape. He seemed to have the least reaction of any of them. Not angry. Not happy. Just a hard to read neutral. She was sure there was more dancing behind those green eyes than he was letting on.

They seemed to be presenting a united front. So they were all in on and into this little plan. What a pack of sickos.

Rex was talking again.

"You'll do as you're told, when you're told to do it.

You'll make yourself available to any one of us. You'll be ours. And in return, we'll make sure nobody captures you, tortures you, and kills you. Sound like a deal?"

Lacey straightened her shoulders, looked him dead in the eye, and answered, "No deal."

For a second, she thought she saw disappointment in his eyes. Did he really expect her to take that deal? Did any of them? As she glared at them, they did all seem a little deflated, except for Mr. Angry.

"Well, Miss Christie, it was nice to see you again, we wish you all the very best," Rex said. He was either calling what he hoped was a bluff, or they were actually going to leave her to her fate.

Whizzzzzzzip!

A bullet sang through the window, skimmed past her cheek, and slammed into the cinder block wall just inches from her head. Lacey screamed and threw herself down, finding herself immediately covered by two very large bodies. In spite of the fact they were ready to leave her to die a second earlier, every single one of them threw himself to her defense without question. Col and Max ran out the door, guns at the ready and Chase and Brian were hunkered over her while Rex barked orders.

There was shouting, running, squealing tires. Whoever had taken the shot didn't want to be run down and caught. The entire incident lasted maybe thirty seconds, but it left her trembling on the bed, tears in her eyes. They were really trying to kill her, and they'd found her. She wasn't going to last ten seconds without these men to help. If they hadn't been there... Lacey couldn't bring herself to think about it.

Chase pulled her up and pressed his thumb to her cheek. "Small graze," he breathed. "You just got the kind of lucky most people don't get twice."

There were six people in the room. The guys had been lined up like sitting ducks next to the window. If it had been random, one of them would have been easy to take out. But nobody wanted them. That bullet had been meant for her.

"Rex," Chase said, his voice desperate. "We can't leave her."

"She doesn't want our help," Mr. Angry said as he returned to the room, still brimming with rage. Then the rest of them began to chime in, talking over one another.

"Of course she didn't agree to that!"

"Maybe she doesn't have a choice."

Rex looked at Lacey coldly as he had the final say. "Take her."

It happened far faster than Lacey could react. All four of them aside from Rex grabbed her, pushed her face down on the bed, and pulled her arms behind her back. They were fastened a second later with what felt like a thick band of plastic. A similar device was wrapped around her ankles. Cable ties. She was being taken prisoner.

Lacey was so scared and confused she didn't even scream as her rescuers turned into her captors. A second later, a pillowcase went over her head and the whole world went beige.

CHAPTER THREE

Brian

"We can't just take her…" Brian glanced over his shoulder with a worried look. They had, in fact, just taken her and were burning down the road at the maximum allowable speed, heading for state lines. This was about as much of an abduction as an abduction could be.

"Of course we can, when the alternative is her being shot dead in a motel," Max said, gnawing on a stick of candy cigarette. He had given up smoking five years earlier, but the candy cigarette addiction was harder to beat.

"Well, I mean, what Rex said, about her being ours. Saying that she had to do whatever we wanted…"

"We're not rapists," Max said bluntly.

"I know! But what he said…"

"Rex offered her a deal she didn't take," Max shrugged.

"But she's still ours though. We've got her."

"Jesus, Brains. What are you getting at?"

"I mean, obviously, we're not going to do anything she doesn't want."

"Right. Obviously."

"But right now she's in a cage, and she probably doesn't

want that."

"That's for her own protection," Max smirked. "And it's not a cage. It's a transit protection enclosure."

He mimicked Brian's voice, hearkening back to when they'd had the thing installed in the vehicle, and Brian had gone around insisting that the cage wasn't a cage, and pointing out all the features that made it a TPE.

Brian rolled his eyes and ignored Max. He was worried. For a lot of reasons. Two main ones though.

One, like Col and the others, he had his reservations about helping Lacey too. She'd gotten them all in a lot of trouble last time, even if she hadn't meant to. She was impulsive, she liked to stick her nose in where it didn't belong, and she had a big mouth. A natural journalist, in other words, but not an ideal companion for a mercenary group.

Two, she was attractive. Very, very attractive. And none of them really had a chance to form relationships with women, not meaningful ones because they were never in the same place for long. It was hard to maintain a relationship with anyone when you would disappear for weeks at a time without explanation, or sometimes, even any notice. To say that she was trapped with five very oversexed men was an understatement. Brian just couldn't see how this ended well for any of them.

CHAPTER FOUR

Lacey

"Let me out!" Lacey yelled through her pillowcase. She was being bumped about in what felt like the hard trunk of a car, though it was too spacious to be a trunk. Must be the back of the behemoth vehicle they'd brought to her motel room.

"Shh!" Chase said from somewhere close by. "Settle down, you're fine."

His voice was soothing, but she was demonstrably not fine. She was tied up in the back of a speeding vehicle, having just barely escaped an assassination attempt with her life, in the company of five men who had just announced an intention to take her as their slave.

"Let me out!"

"Gag her."

She recognized Angry's voice.

"Leave her be, Col."

That's right. His name was Col. Not short for Colin. Just Col. He'd been distant years ago, and he was outright hostile now. Col had the slightest hint of a British clip to his tone. Her journalistic mind made a note to investigate that more.

The rest of her panicky, stressed mind took control of her vocal cords again.

"Please! Let me go!"

"Brian, stop the van." It was Rex's drawl that made the vehicle come to a halt. Lacey squirmed around, not knowing where the doors were until she heard them squeak open behind her. Strong hands grasped her by the hips and turned her around. A second later, the pillowcase was pulled off her head. She found herself looking into Rex's stern gaze. He had something dark in his hand, something he unrolled as he looked at her.

"What are you doing to me? You have to let me go. Please."

"Nope," Rex said simply. "Open your mouth."

She shut it firmly.

"I can force it in, and it will hurt, or you can open your mouth and it won't," he said.

"Please," she begged. "Don't do this. I don't want this."

"We're doing our job regardless. You called us, remember?"

"Well, I didn't think…"

"No, of course you didn't." Rex spoke shortly, his Texan drawl bringing an incongruous charm to his lecture. "You didn't think when you got yourself caught in Venezuela. You didn't think when you told our business to the world, and you didn't think when you called Chase. You don't think, little girl. You talk. And I've had about enough of that, so you're going to wear this gag until I decide otherwise. Now open up."

What choice was there? Lacey parted her lips obediently and true to his word, Rex wasn't as rough as he could have been. He pushed the cloth into her mouth and wound it around her head several times before tying it at the back of her head. She couldn't speak, but it didn't hurt. He gave her a satisfied look, then shut the cage again and walked back around the van. It was a small mercy that he didn't put the pillowcase back over her head, so now she could at least see.

She sat there, totally helpless as they set off again. From her view through the mesh, it looked like Brian was driving with Max in the passenger seat. Rex and Col were in the middle seats. Chase was at the back just in front of her. She could have whispered to him if it wasn't for the gag.

This wasn't safe. She didn't have a seatbelt. If they crashed, she was fucked. She made a mental note to tear strips off them once they stopped. Not just for the seatbelt. That was kind of minor in the grand scheme of kidnapping. Satisfied that she was going to at least do something about her situation, she settled down and glared at the backs of their heads as they turned off the main road and started heading down a gravel track.

CHAPTER FIVE

Chase

It took several hours for them to reach safety. It was a long drive, but long drives were good drives when it came to losing tails. They had taken a very long roundabout way to ensure that they didn't have one—although not seeing one wasn't the same as not having one.

Their safe house sat on the border with Virginia. It was a small cabin set in rural forest farmland that hid a lot of the high-tech surveillance equipment that kept it secure. It was one of a dozen such houses they had across the country. They'd be secure there, with any luck, though Brian was going to have to monitor traffic and chatter around the area for a while to make sure.

As soon as they pulled up outside the cabin, Chase jumped out of the van and went to the back. He wanted to take care of Lacey. He owed her that much. This was already well out of hand. Rex's conditions for helping her were extreme, but in Chase's view, necessary. Lacey was in a desperately dangerous situation, and that meant everyone near her would be in danger too. For the second time in three years, she'd been minutes away from death. They couldn't keep bailing her out of these situations. She needed supervision of the closest kind, and she'd get it with them.

He threw open the back door and saw her sitting curled up in the corner. She looked so pitiful with the black cloth wrapped around her mouth. Pitiful, helpless, and hot.

Truth was, Chase hadn't given it a second thought when she called asking for help. Lacey had been on his mind since Venezuela. Yeah, she'd gotten them fired, but she hadn't been the one to fire them and he didn't blame her entirely. That had been a shitty chain of command that didn't want to take responsibility for their own ops.

A case could be made that it wasn't actually Lacey's fault. In fact, she'd probably saved their lives. Mercenary work was dangerous, but they could choose their assignments and ameliorate much more of the risk. Nobody sent them running into gunfire, or used them as meat puppets. And they made a hell of a lot more money now than they ever had in the service. Money wasn't everything, but mixed with freedom and safety, it added up.

"C'mere," he said, reaching for her. Easiest way to carry her was over his shoulder so he scooped her neat little body up that way and took her into the house, grinning to himself as he took her shapely form over the threshold. Lacey was looking good. She'd cleaned up really nicely after being a Venezuelan prisoner. She had definitely not been at her best when he found her three years ago. It was nice to see her again. Really nice. He was looking forward to her settling in and starting to enjoy their company. The prospect of sharing her with the others was a bit of a challenge though. Ideally, he'd have her for himself, but Lacey was far too much for any one man to handle. You left her alone for a few minutes and she organized a revolution. Five men sounded about right. Four maybe, if Col kept up his sniping.

The cabin was set out more or less open plan. There was a kitchen / dining / lounge area that contained the usual furniture. Nothing fancy. It hadn't been interior designed. It had just been filled with what they needed. Bedrooms ran off down a hall adjacent. He was tempted to take her there, but Rex was already tapping him on the shoulder.

"Chase, I need you. Get her in a chair."

Chase lowered Lacey into a simple wood chair near the couch and leaned down. "Don't worry," he said, hoping he was being comforting. "We'll get you settled soon."

She made muffled noises. He knew what she wanted. There was no need for her to be gagged now, and hell, the restraints were probably overkill too. He crouched down in front of her, pulled the plastic from her legs, and moved up her body.

"Keep her secure," Col said. "I'm not chasing her all over the woods if she makes a break for it."

Chase cut him a dark look. "She's been bound for hours. Ease up."

Col shot a dirty glower right back at him. "No."

Chase undid her hands as well, snapping through the plastic with his knife. Lacey made a sound of relief and rubbed her wrists. There were red marks on her skin where the ties had been a little tight.

"I said, secure her," Col growled. "Or I will."

"Get her tied up, Chase!" Rex called out from across the room. He was setting up tactical charts on the kitchen table. "I need you."

"Got rope? Cable ties are too harsh."

Lacey was watching him with silent judgment, her pretty brown eyes filled with palpable betrayal. He couldn't blame her for hating him. She hadn't expected this. She'd thought he'd come alone, a knight in shining armor. But one knight wasn't going to cut it. A damsel in this much distress needed a whole platoon.

Chase put his fingers to his lips indicating she should be quiet as he reached up and removed the gag. She managed to stay silent, and he nodded in approval. Good girl. She could follow instructions.

Col went off to the back somewhere. When he returned, he handed Chase a length of hemp and Chase used it to bind

Lacey securely to the chair. She squirmed beneath his hands, her curves reluctantly accepting the bindings. She was in good shape, which made sense given the amount of running for her life she had to do. He could only imagine how much trouble she'd managed to get into in the last three years.

"You've got to be kidding me," she complained as he secured her.

"Stay quiet," he said. "You don't want the gag again, do you?"

She fell silent, but it was not a happy silence. It was a barely compliant silence. Chase was starting to think that the rope was probably a good idea. She looked like she was about to bolt, even with the black hemp wrapped around her arms and waist and looping under her breasts. She had a nice chest. Chase tried not to stare, but there was just something about a bound woman that made his blood run hotter.

"Chase?" Rex called him again. "Now."

"Coming."

CHAPTER SIX

Lacey

Lacey sat in the chair they'd tied her to and tried to work out if she was any safer here than she would have been with the people looking to kill her. Col was prowling the room like a caged beast, Brian was on his laptop. Rex and Chase and Max were in deep conversation in the far corner. Something important was happening over there, apparently. She would have liked to have been a part of it, but obviously they had no intention of including her.

She was uncomfortable. Being tied up wasn't nice, and after having been bound in the vehicle she had been looking forward to stretching her legs and being able to work some of her nerves off. Tied to a chair, she was left to basically vibrate, her knee bouncing as she tapped her feet.

"Stay still," Col said as he walked past. He seemed irritated by her mere presence. She shot him a dirty look and kept doing what she was doing as he orbited around her. He was telling her off for doing the same thing he was trying to do, burning off excess energy.

"I need to pee," she said as he came past on yet another unnecessary patrol.

He shot her a cold look. "Hold it."

"I have been," she protested. "I can't anymore."

"Then go in the chair."

She glared at him. Fuck this guy. Unlike her, nobody had forced him to come.

"You can just leave," she said. "I don't need you if you're going to be like this."

She saw rage flash in his eyes, as if he couldn't believe she had the nerve to say that to him. Lacey didn't care. He didn't look like he was interested in helping. He didn't even look like he was interested in Rex's weirdly perverse idea of them all owning her somehow. She saw his hand flex, as if he was thinking of hitting her, and a bolt of nerves went through her belly. She wouldn't be able to protect herself if he did. She was tied up tight, totally defenseless.

"You are damn lucky you and I aren't alone," he told her before stalking off to the other side of the room.

"Uhm, Chase!" she called out.

"What is it?" Chase lifted his head from the little conference on the other side of the cabin.

"I need to use the bathroom."

"Take her, Col."

Col glanced over at her and Lacey blanched.

"Not him. Anyone but him."

"Brian. Can you take her?"

"I'm working out coordinates for hundreds of cars to make sure we weren't followed," Brian said without lifting his eyes from the screen of his laptop. "You really want me to stop for a potty break?"

"Col or hold it," Chase said.

She elected to hold it.

Col watched as she squirmed in the chair. She didn't know how long she could hold it, but she was going to as long as possible. There was no way she was going to ask Col to take her to the bathroom. She'd rather wet herself.

As it turned out, the choice was taken out of her hands. After another couple minutes of her increasingly desperate squirming, Col lost patience.

"Come on," he growled, yanking the ropes partially off her. He pulled her up and out of the chair and marched her to the bathroom. Her hands were still bound, so he grabbed her pants for her and pulled them down in a swift motion before seating her on the toilet.

"What the hell!"

"You need to go. So go."

The door was open. He was watching. He'd just gotten her half naked like it wasn't anything at all, and now he expected her to pee on command like a dog. Worst thing was, she really needed to go, and she didn't know if she could hold it.

She felt her face flush with pure humiliation.

"Shut the door."

"Nope."

"Why?"

"Someone could come in the window if we don't have eyes on you. Eyes on at all times."

"You want to watch me take a dump?"

"I don't want to watch you at all," he said, his lip curling in derision. "But I'm going to anyway."

She couldn't hold it anymore. A few drops escaped her and then once she started she couldn't stop, the sound of the hot stream hitting the water making her blush furiously. Worse still, she'd needed to go to the toilet so bad it took what felt like forever to empty her bladder. On and on she peed, Col's brows rising as the never-ending trickle carried on.

"Undo my hands," she said when she was finally done. "I need to wipe."

He grabbed the toilet paper. She recoiled as best she could.

"No! Not you!"

"Chase!" Col called out. "Come wipe your princess' precious butt!"

She burned with embarrassment as Chase came over and

saw her in the position Col had put her in.

"What did you want me to do? Let her go unsecured just to pee?" Col defended himself before any questions had been asked.

"Just undo my hands," she begged. "I'm not going to do anything stupid."

Chase hesitated, then got behind her and yanked the rope off.

"Get yourself cleaned up," he said. "Quickly."

He didn't close the door either, but he did at least turn his back so she had some privacy as she wiped and pulled her pants up and flushed the toilet.

She hated Col with a passion.

"Thanks," she said after washing her hands. She cupped some water and splashed it onto her face to refresh herself. The bathroom mirror showed Chase watching her, an inscrutable expression on his handsome face.

"Why does Col have to be here?"

"Because there's five of us and a lot more of them. We need every man we can get. Just don't antagonize him, okay?"

"I didn't! He was antagonizing me!" she protested as Chase took her by the arm and escorted her out of the bathroom.

"Sit down next to Brains and keep quiet," he said, pushing her down on the soft couch. He walked back to Rex and Max, returning to whatever work they were doing. Col had retired to the kitchen and seemed to be making a sandwich. Good. At least he was out of her face.

"Hey," she murmured to Brian.

"Hey," he replied, a dimpled smile on his lips. He didn't actually look at her, but he didn't seem to be unhappy that she was there.

If this was a wolf pack, Brian would be the omega. But oh, what an omega he was. *Elegant*, that was the word that sprang to mind, closely followed by *deadly*. He was the closest to her age, and she liked to think they could have been friends.

She sat in silence for a few minutes as he tapped away, absorbed in his work. As she looked around the room, she realized someone was missing.

"Wasn't there another one?"

"Fraser died last year." Brains said it without inflection. Just a piece of information.

Oh, shit. She felt guilty right away.

"I'm sorry."

Brian didn't say anything, just kept typing.

Was it her fault? Had she already gotten one of them killed somehow?

She sat there, running her palms over her thighs nervously. This was getting out of hand. She had to do something. Say something. She had to fix this, somehow.

Lacey stood up and cleared her throat. "Uhm, guys?"

Five pairs of eyes turned toward her. She felt her entire body hum with nervousness. She barely knew these men. The rescue mission had taken three days and they'd been too busy escaping militia groups to really get to know one another beyond the superficial.

"I'm sorry I brought you all into this," she said. "I should have kept my mouth shut and just…"

"Died today?" Max spoke up, his scruffy wild brows drawing down over his eyes.

"Well…"

"That's what would have happened," Max said bluntly. "You'd be dead. Bullet to the brain. Done."

"Well, uhm…"

She fell silent for a second, feeling stupid for having opened her mouth. She should probably sit down, but she couldn't leave it at that.

"Brian told me about Fraser and… I'm sorry. I didn't know I'd lead to someone's death. You got me out of danger. I can take it from here. Thank you for everything, and I'm sorry for everything I did. I wish I could go back, but it's too late. I can never make it up to you. I know that.

I should never have called…"

Their expressions ranged from confused, to compassionate, to steadily more annoyed.

"Fraser had cancer," Chase said. "That wasn't your fault."

"One of the very few things that isn't," Col snorted. His derision oddly made her feel better. She had been getting pretty sure she was responsible for everything from the Suez crisis to the impending heat death of the universe in Col's eyes.

"Oh. I'm so sorry," she said, the corners of her mouth turning down. "I owe him my life as much as I owe the rest of you. But the rest of what I said applies. Just leave me. I'll get by somehow." She forced what she hoped was a brave smile.

"No." It was Rex who spoke decisively. "There's no going back now, Lacey."

"You said it," Max chimed in. "Can't undo what's done. You can't undo selling that story, and we won't leave you to die. You're stuck with us."

She smiled a little. She thought she could probably handle being stuck with Chase and Max and Brian. It was Rex and Col who gave her serious reservations.

"Well, not all of you need to stay here," she said. "I mean, you must have actual work to do."

"We do," Rex said. "You'll have to be put somewhere safe when we're doing that."

Somewhere safe. That sounded nice, but she was sure that it wouldn't be.

Brian reached up, grabbed her shirt, and tugged her back down next to him. "Let them work."

It was a simple order, one that showed he was not as omega as she had imagined him to be. He just had a different, quieter, absolutely confident style of dominance.

She sat down, feeling embarrassed and somehow small. These were serious men with serious jobs and she had just become a tag-along, an inconvenience in their lives.

"We should put her away," Col said in between bites of sandwich. "Don't want her hearing or seeing anything she can report on."

"I'm not going to do that! I would never do that... again," she added lamely.

Brian snorted next to her. Okay, so maybe none of them had really forgiven her or were okay with her. Maybe some of them were just quieter about it than others.

"Okay, you know what? I don't have to sit here and take this," she said, standing up and moving toward the door. "I'm leaving. Thanks for everything..."

The floor went out from under her as she was tackled by not one, but two large men. Col and Brian both had her, their arms under her shoulders. She started to kick and scream, but Col's hard hand was slapped over her mouth as they pinned her down on the couch and started trussing her again, tape over her mouth, rope around her arms and legs.

She panicked, utterly terrified, a high-pitched sound escaping her in spite of the tape as her heart hammered in her chest. The bindings were even tighter than they had been before and she couldn't take it. Not again. She'd barely been able to tolerate being in the back of the van, and then in the chair. She was fast reaching the end of her personal tether for being tied up.

Chase was the only one to really notice or care how stressed it made her. As Brian and Col left her flailing on the couch, he came forward to soothe her.

"You've got to calm down, sweetheart," Chase said, stroking her hair gently away from her forehead. "We're not going to hurt you, but..."

"Oh, we're going to hurt her," Col chimed in. "We're just not going to harm her."

"Shut the hell up, Col," Chase growled. "You're not helping."

"I'm not going to make this easy on her. She didn't make it easy on us!"

"I said, shut up!" Chase stood to face his comrade. They

were practically nose to nose, growling at one another like two fierce big cats as Lacey watched, helplessly bound.

"Break it up!" Rex walked through the middle of the muscular men, shoving them both aside "If you're going to fight over her, she goes in the cage."

Lacey shook her head furiously. No. Not the cage. She didn't want to be alone in the vehicle, even if it was air conditioned.

"We're not fighting, we're…"

"Okay, that's it."

She let out a squeal as Rex stooped and grabbed her up before carrying her away, not to the car as she had been afraid of, but through a door she had figured led to a closet or something. Except it didn't.

There was a big iron cage behind that door—or a small prison cell. She had technically been held in worse, but that didn't mean this was okay, because it wasn't. She started to scream through the tape, kicking and wriggling, but Rex didn't pay any mind to her struggles. He put her down on a fold-out cot that sat inside and crouched to pull the ropes off her before removing the tape, which stung as he peeled it from her soft lips. Tied and untied, tied and untied, she couldn't keep up with the rapid fire bondage.

"Please don't leave me in here," she begged as soon as she could speak, tears filling her eyes. "Please. Seriously. I'll do anything."

"Anything except sit down, be quiet, and stay out of the way," Rex said simply. "You brought this on yourself, little girl. You've got to stop winding my boys up."

"But I'm not!"

"You are, with your speeches, and trying to walk out and all the rest of it. You're a woman, Lacey, and nothing sends a unit haywire quicker than an undisciplined female."

"Please," she begged. "Do anything else. Don't leave me in here."

He looked at her, his hard eyes on her tear-filled ones. Maybe he thought she was trying to play on his kindness—

as if she thought he had any. She wasn't pretending. The cage scared her deeply. She'd spent time in captivity before, and she never wanted to again. After Venezuela, she couldn't handle confined spaces. Even bathroom stalls could send her into a panicked spin.

"Alright. Well, there's one way to change that undisciplined factor." He winked. It was an incongruous jolt of sudden friendliness and it threw her off completely.

She wasn't sure what he meant and there wasn't time to ask as he got up and sat on the cot bed beside her. It was only a few inches off the floor, so his long legs sprawled easily to the other side of the cage. She looked at him curiously, not knowing what his plan was, even when he took hold of her and tipped her over his thighs.

"What!" Her squeak of shock sounded almost cartoonish as his big hand covered her legging-clad ass.

"Little girls who don't behave themselves need to be spanked," Rex said, his deep mature voice running through her. She couldn't believe it. This wasn't happening. If he'd just thrown her into the cell and walked away leaving her sobbing behind him, that would have made sense than this.

"What are you doing?"

CHAPTER SEVEN

Rex

What was he doing? Exactly what he needed to do, that was what.

Seeing Lacey in that motel room a few hours ago had been like seeing a new person. The dirty, beaten wretch they'd rescued from the Venezuelan militia had been replaced with a beautifully vibrant young woman with more attitude in her little finger than most people had in their entire bodies. She'd always had courage, but back when they'd first found her she'd been in such a desperate state and they'd been in such a tense and dangerous situation that there really wasn't any time to appreciate her. They hadn't even been sure that she'd survived until her story came out—and soon their troubles had started.

She squirmed, confused. Most people would know what this position meant, but it figured she'd never been spanked in her life. No matter how much danger she was in, she maintained a sort of naivety that could only come from a formative period free of consequences.

He didn't have time to put her insubordinate butt through boot camp and teach her about the concepts of chain of command. He needed to get her under control quickly. Seemed to him, a good spanking would probably get the message through to her easier than any other method.

"We're going to get a few things straight here," he drawled. "I can't have you acting out."

"I wasn't!"

"Girl, you don't even know what acting out is," he said. He liked that he had her attention, and he hadn't even touched her round little butt. "In my book, it's anything that goes against orders you've been given by any one of us. I don't care which one. If someone tells you to sit your ass down, you sit down. If someone tells you to be quiet, you don't open your mouth. In fact, little girl, to make it easy, you don't speak unless you're spoken to, understand?"

Her spluttered little gasp told him she hadn't, so he followed it up with a firm slap, catching both her generous cheeks with his palm.

"Ow!"

Rex knew for certain she'd endured more pain than what he was giving her right now. The Venezuelan militia had worked her over for sure. A little tap on the butt was nothing to a girl like her, and yet her yelp, high-pitched and surprised, sounded genuine.

"Are you following me, Lacey?"

"Yessir!"

He melted at the unprompted *sir*. Goddamn. She was adorable. She was also a catalyst for chaos. He couldn't forget that, even with her cute legging-clad ass squirming over his thighs.

He slapped her ass again, enjoying the way her soft full cheeks jiggled under his palm. Repeating the treatment several more times, he made sure to whack the fullest part of her bottom. The sound was satisfying, both the slap of his hand meeting her ass, and the little gasps and squeaks she was making. She deserved a really good long hard one of these for betraying them, but that would come another time. Right now, he didn't have the time to give her the kind of care she was going to need after he spanked her properly.

"I'm giving you one more chance, little girl," he growled down at her. "Remember, not a word unless someone speaks to you. You go sit down and you stay sitting down until you get another order. If you break either one of those rules, I'm going to do this properly. Understand?"

"Yessir!"

"I mean it," he repeated. "This is your one and only warning."

"I understand, sir," she sniffed.

Rex and Chase and the others had shared a lot of long talks about this young woman over the last three years. They'd often talked about what they'd do if they could get their hands on her. Tanning her ass had been pretty low down on the list. Most of it had been a lot rougher than this.

He gave her butt another hard slap, just to satisfy himself, but he could already imagine the looks he'd get from his men, especially Col. If he stopped now they wouldn't think he'd gone far enough. Maybe he hadn't. Couldn't let them think he was going to go soft on her. Couldn't let her think he was going to go soft on her either. This tightrope of holding respect without being a monster was one he'd been walking for a long time, but sometimes it was difficult as hell.

CHAPTER EIGHT

Lacey

She really shouldn't be enjoying this. Of all the outrageous things that had happened to her today this had to be the worst, barring the bullet through the window, oh, and the toilet… okay, this wasn't even close to registering by today's standards. On the scale of a normal day though, being held over an older man's knee and spanked was an outrage. She just couldn't muster any though. This was the nicest thing that had happened in a while, even though her butt stung.

He was trying to discipline her, she knew that. But Lacey hadn't been snugged up against a man's body in a while, and she'd never experienced anything like this, a stern but ultimately relatively gentle discipline. She was grateful that he was sparing her the dreaded cage and as much as being slapped hurt, it also made her press against him for comfort.

As she squirmed, she felt something hard against her hip. Something hard and masculine that reminded her abruptly of what he'd said to her before the bullet. Something about being theirs. All of theirs. At the time she'd reacted with horror, but right now, with her ass hot and a squirming sensation low in her belly, it didn't seem as awful a prospect.

His large hand splayed out over her ass, a protective and possessive touch. Then she felt his fingers curling in the hem of her pants, pulling them down. Slowly. Very slowly.

She made a little motion and his other hand went to the back of her head, his fingers curling in her hair.

"Stay still," he growled as he peeled her leggings and underwear down together inch by inch. Taking his time, making her feel every little bit of progressive exposure. Her hips swayed with instinctive motion as she drew in a deep breath, taking his scent in. Masculine tinged with a hint of cologne.

Rex was an intimidating man. A hard man, but he was handling her with a skilled gentleness that made her start to consider the possibility that being his, and maybe even being theirs wouldn't be the absolute worst thing in the world. Or maybe that was just stress and arousal talking, making her think crazy things. She didn't know. All she really knew was that her clothing was halfway down her ass and lowering steadily.

The little room was really a renovated closet, so it wasn't as if she and Rex had any real privacy in there. Everyone would have heard and seen her be spanked, and now they were almost certainly seeing her bare ass come into view.

She blushed, glad that she was facing toward the far wall and that she didn't have to see them looking at her, though she could feel the masculine eyes devouring her rear as Rex pushed the spandex and cotton below her ass and then kept pushing them down until they settled at mid-thigh. It wasn't just her butt on display. It was everything. They would be seeing her pussy, the dark little curls that she hadn't manicured in some time protecting her lower lips.

"Naughty girls get spanked on the bare," Rex said gruffly. He put his hand on her bottom and a bolt of pure electricity shot through her as she felt his flesh meeting hers. Goddamn. Being touched felt good. Really good.

Maybe it was just the adrenaline from being shot at and

then captured and driven around as a captive. Maybe it was stress. Whatever it was, her senses were exceptionally heightened. She was more sensitive than she had ever been, and the feeling of his hard hand against her tender ass made inner parts of her person clench in a way that betrayed everything she'd had to say on the subject so far.

Rex was a dangerous man. A mercenary. She'd taken his career from him and now he had her pinned with her pants down over his lap and was punishing her. His hand moved away and she let out a little squeak, anticipating serious pain and agony.

"I didn't even spank you yet," he guffawed before bringing his palm swinging down against her ass with a firm swat that made her yelp for real. He repeated the act another dozen times, his hand meeting her lower cheeks over and over again, catching the fullest part of her ass. There was no accident to that, she was sure. Even as pain and heat bloomed through her body, she knew she was in the hands of a man who knew how to make it hurt just like he wanted it to.

The harder and longer he spanked, the more the sensation built, making her writhe over his lap. His other hand didn't leave her hair, keeping her in place as he whacked her into a frenzy of yelps and yells, her ass heating, rising and falling over his thighs, her pussy pounding against the ridge of his leg, clit grinding every time she made contact.

He was thrashing her, not because she'd done anything wrong right now, but because he could. She could feel his desire rampant in his pants, pressing against her thigh as she ground up and down, her legs spreading as much as they could inside her spandex hobbles.

"Jesus," somebody growled from behind. She could only imagine the sight her swollen red ass made as it bounced over Rex's lap. Lewd. Obscene. Filthy. Rex had stripped her of her underwear and of the last vestige of dignity. She'd been thinking that maybe he would set things straight, make

LOKI RENARD

it so Col and the others treated her with a little more respect—but she saw now that had been utterly naive. It was Rex who was leading this mission. He was the one who was going to make her bend to their will, and if she didn't bend, she would be punished. He'd told her all these things without saying a word.

"You're going to be ours, Lacey, whether you like it or not."

"Yes," she hissed, even though a question hadn't been asked. Rex wasn't just spanking her ass anymore; his fingers were flaring out and catching her pussy too. Their swiping slaps should have hurt a lot more, but her pussy was reacting to the spanking in a way she couldn't believe. She was wet. And not just a little wet. A lot wet. Every time his fingers caught her sensitive lips, they took a smear of her juices with them.

She started to let out little squeals of pain and pleasure too as the slaps to her pussy became less plausibly deniable and more deliberate. He rubbed her pussy for a second, his hot, hard fingers brushing over her swelling lower lips before he spanked it directly, his fingers catching her lips and her clit too.

"Ooo!" Lacey squealed. She could feel him hardening even more against her thigh as her hips danced over his lap. She couldn't help herself. He was driving her into a frenzy of pleasure pain that did not allow for anything but honest animal reaction.

Something was building between them. Something that would not be denied. In any other place, and in any other time, she would have been shocked and stunned to be held down and have her ass and pussy spanked. But here, it felt right. More than that, it felt necessary. She needed this. Every bit of it. And as the tension grew and her sore little pussy got wetter, something broke.

"Fuck it," Rex growled.

He pushed her off his thigh, his hand keeping control of her head as he spun her around on her knees and pushed

42

her belly first down on the bed. She heard a zipper and then felt the hot head of his bare cock, skin on skin at the very apex of her legs, her slick wet pussy betraying any attempt to repel him as he pushed forward.

He was going to fuck her.

Lacey screamed as his cock plundered her cunt, her inner walls spreading for him. Thrust after thrust, his hips found her sore spanked ass, slapping against it in a new way that reignited the earlier slaps and reminded her that she was being punished. She was also being fucked. Hard. And publicly. She screamed into the scratchy military blanket as Rex pounded inside her, his hand fisting the back of her head.

She'd never been fucked like this before. Never been taken by a man who wanted her so much he was willing to dispense with every barrier between them without warning. Pure lust drove them both into a frenzy of animal desire as Lacey arched her hips back, offering her tight cunt to the dominant man who owned her in every sense of the word that mattered. His cock stretched her over and over again, that hard rod swelling inside her.

Lacey knew what those twitches and that thickening meant. Her orgasm was close, but his was even closer. He wasn't doing what men usually did, trying to hold back to make it last longer for her pleasure. He was fucking her because he wanted to fuck her, and he was going to come because that was the purpose of fucking a nice tight cunt.

"I'm not on birth control," she gasped.

"I don't care."

His growl shocked her as he shoved himself deep and came inside her, his seed flooding her bare pussy. He jolted his hips against her sore ass, making sure every single drop was trapped inside her.

Stunned, Lacey laid there, her pussy full of cum. He'd fucked and filled her and the consequences didn't matter. She was his little fuck hole to use. He held himself deep inside her, his thick cock pulsing those last spurts of cum against the very entrance of her womb. This was madness, but he didn't care and she didn't have a choice. Her inner walls were grasping his cock, drawing everything he had to give as deep as possible.

After a minute or so, Rex pulled himself out of her and left her dripping as he set about pulling her pants off completely, then yanking her shoes off too. She was left in her tank top, sports bra, and her socks. Rex picked her up, not by her arm or around her waist, but with one strong arm looping around her body and reaching between her thighs. The other went around under her breasts as he hoisted her aloft and carried her back out into the living area where the other four were standing in a sort of stunned arousal. She could barely meet their eyes, but she knew that every eye in the place was locked on her.

"I've broken her in. You'll all have your turn," Rex said, his hand cupping her messy pussy, his fingers soaked with her juices and his cum. "But you'll earn it. Every one of her holes has a price."

"A price?" Lacey gasped. She was the only one who seemed shocked by the proposition.

"I'm trying to save you from being fucked into oblivion," he growled in her ear. "If we five have free rein of you, you're going to be rode hard every damn minute of the day, and I don't think your sweet little cunt can take that."

She gulped in agreement, even as her pussy clenched at the words. She was still riding the orgasmic wave of illicit excitement, and it left her wanting more. He'd torn away the very last semblances of propriety from her. He'd reduced her to a quivering cum-filled mess. Maybe it was the fact that she knew she was lucky to be alive, but the outrage she should have been feeling wasn't anywhere near her radar. This was living as she had never lived before. This was rough and raw and so damn real.

"Her mouth is two thousand. Her pussy is five thousand. Her ass is ten."

Lacey's eyes went wide at the prices. Thousands? Surely she wasn't worth that to any of them. Surely they'd refuse. Especially Chase. Dear, sweet knight in shining armor Chase. She couldn't see him agreeing to something this debased.

They all nodded, except for Col, who just shrugged. "What does the money go toward?"

"Goes toward keeping her alive," Rex said. "It's going to cost a hell of a lot, and I reckon user pays is the best system."

"Good," Col said. "This way I don't have to pay for her bullshit."

She was actually grateful to him. Now she only had four cocks to worry about. God. Four cocks. This was not how she had anticipated this day going at all. Her pussy was tender and aching beneath Rex's fingers even as he lowered her to the floor, taking the pressure off her pounded pussy. He kept his hand there though, rubbing her creamy slit in a way that made it impossible for her to think straight.

"What about machines?" Brian asked the question mildly.

The others laughed.

"Depends on the hole you take, you sick little fuck," Rex chuckled. "Same price for your machines as for your dick."

Machines? What the hell were they talking about?

"Put me down for two thousand," Max said, stepping forward. "I want her mouth now."

"Suck his cock," Rex ordered, pushing her to her knees.

Propelled by a force much stronger than her, Lacey sank down, Rex's cum still sliding out of her as Max pulled his thick, hard, uncut cock from his pants.

"That was hot," he told her. "I want to see you take this."

Lacey hesitated, a little spark of sense frantic in her mind. If she did this she'd be agreeing to their little scheme. She'd be agreeing to fuck for her life. That made her, what, a prostitute? No. Prostitutes got money for sex. She was getting protection. Still, it was a blatant transaction.

"I don't have to do this. You already said you wouldn't let me go, so you're not going to kick me out if I say no."

"You don't have to agree to this," Rex agreed. "I'm sure we can work out some other means of sharing you."

"I can say no?"

"You can," Rex confirmed.

"I mean, you can…" Max said hopefully. "But yes would be nice."

Max was a behemoth. Big, muscled like a bull. In Venezuela she'd seen him go through three militia men, body armor absorbing their blows as he charged through them as if they weren't even there. His cock was sized to suit, a big thick member that would fill her mouth to stretching if he were to push it past her lips.

Col snorted derisively. Chase was watching with an interested gaze. Brian had gone back to tapping furiously at the computer. Rex was behind her, hands on her shoulders. He wasn't holding her down, he was just guiding her.

She let her gaze fall on the thick cock, her tongue extending just a little to lick around her lips. She was tempted to do this. Rex put his hand on the back of her head and urged her forward just a little, bringing her mouth to the tip of Max's cock.

He let out a groan and she felt her pussy quiver in response. Max was fucking hot, and her well fucked pussy wasn't entirely satisfied just yet. This was a kind of arousal she hadn't felt before. She'd been horny, of course. She'd wanted to fuck. But usually once the act was over, she was done. Not now. Right now her body was humming with erotic energy, charged with the excitement of danger.

"Good girl," Rex purred as he pushed her head forward, impaling her mouth on Max's cock. She took several inches in one slow stroke that she did not control in the slightest. It was Rex who was in charge, easing her down on Max's cock time and time again, pushing her head a little further forward every time, her lips and tongue enveloping the throbbing thick flesh.

She risked a glance at Chase, wondering if he was jealous. She saw pure lust on his handsome face. Of all the men she thought she'd fuck out of this unit, he was the one she'd thought she'd have. Instead, it was Rex's cum dripping from her well used cunt, and Max's cock in her mouth.

"Harder."

Col growled the word. His eyes were narrowed, his teeth clenched. She could see a bulge in his pants. He was aroused, but he was angry. She felt a flutter low in her belly at his rage and wrapped her lips more tightly around Max's cock, lapping her tongue under the head.

She flickered a wink at Col, whose eyes widened even as his lip curled in a sneer. He wanted her to be ashamed? Fuck him. She refused to be ashamed of herself. If this was the price of survival, she'd pay it.

Rex's hands fell away as she drew her head back, licking lightly along the shaft of Max's cock. She wrapped her lips tightly around the head, her eyes locked on Col. Fuck that guy. What a fucking asshole.

Was it possible to suck a cock for revenge? If so, she was doing it.

"Look at me," Max said, grabbing her by the hair. He redirected her gaze to him. She looked up into his eyes, which were locked on her with masculine intensity. He put a second hand on her head, palming either side of her skull, keeping her completely under his control, looking only at him.

Now she wasn't thinking about anything besides him. Now she was his. All his. First Rex, now Max. These men were claiming her completely, freeing her mind from the shackles of fear it had been constrained in for weeks and months. She had not felt one moment of lightness in all that time. The constant threat of danger and death had made it utterly impossible to relax, or to feel good. Doom had dogged her every step.

No longer. Max surged forward, she took his cock, and

hope rose within her as he reminded her what she was in the simplest of ways: a woman, surrounded by men sworn to protect her. His lust ignited both the sparks of her desire, and the simple need to live, to survive, to be fully of the world. Every surge of his hard rod between her lips made her squirm and writhe, her well fucked pussy dripping Rex's seed down her thighs and onto the floor beneath. She was a mess, a wanton, cum-smeared mess and she was about to receive even more.

Max growled and pumped harder, arching his back to thrust deeper. She didn't think she could take his cock any further into her mouth, but as he shoved it to the back of her throat she swallowed and took him even deeper still.

"Fuck!" Max cried out, his cum shooting across her tongue and down her throat as her total submission triggered the most masculine of responses. He came with growls and shouts, his cock twitching and throbbing against her tongue. Shot after shot of his seed filled her mouth until finally his balls were empty and her mouth was full.

He pulled her up from the floor and kissed her passionately, their lips and tongues meeting, his cum shared between them. She felt his protection and his passion as his large arms wrapped around her and held her close, cradling her as if she was something special and precious.

"We're definitely keeping this one," he said to the others as she buried her face against his neck. "Hey, look at me, Lacey."

She looked up into his face, not knowing what he wanted from her, or what to expect from him.

"You did fuck us over," he said. "But I forgive you."

"You do?" Tears filled her eyes. She couldn't believe he was saying that.

"You changed our lives," Max said. "But our lives were never our own anyway. We lived for our country until our country didn't want us anymore. Now, maybe we'll live for something else."

He pushed her hair out of her eyes and dropped another

couple of kisses on her, one on her mouth, the other on her nose.

"You can't forgive me that quickly," she said, stunned.

"Sure I can," Max said. "It's up to me. I don't hold grudges, Lacey. Besides, you're going to have a hard enough time with the others. They're not as forgiving as I am."

"We're not as crazy as you," Chase snorted.

"We're not as stupid," Col growled from the rear.

She tried to turn to him to give him a piece of her mind, but Max caught her in a kiss, capturing her aggressive instincts. His arms wrapped around her and she sank against his hard body, her soft flesh yielding to him and his desire. Lacey had needed this so badly. For just one of them to forgive her, for just one man to show her genuine affection.

"Can I sleep in your bed?" She mumbled the question against his ear. Max was physically the largest of all the men. He could protect her if she needed it.

"No." It was Chase who spoke. "You're in my room tonight."

"How much is she for the night, Rex?" Max asked the question over her head.

"The night? Twenty."

Twenty thousand dollars! There was no way Chase was going to pay that. Even Max had gone for the two thousand dollar option.

Chase looked her dead in the eye. "Done."

CHAPTER NINE

Chase

He wanted her. Alone. He wanted her the way he'd wanted her for years. Twenty thousand was nothing for that. He'd seen the way her eyes went wide every time Rex threw out a number, but they all had large amounts saved up from lucrative mercenary contracts. They all had nice houses, expensive cars, toys of all kinds, but at a certain point, there just weren't enough things to spend money on.

Except Col. Col's money seemed to be like water. The guy was always broke. Not that he'd care. He had about as much interest in Lacey as he had in a viper. That was a direct quote, one of many Col had shared on their way to the motel before they picked up Lacey.

Chase took her gently by the arm and drew her away from Max. "Come on," he said. "Let's go."

She went without resistance. As he led her away down the hall that went to their private rooms he noticed that she smelled of Rex and Max. She smelled used. Their tang hit his nostrils, made his blood rush. He didn't mind sharing her. He was asking them all to put their lives on the line to protect her. But that didn't mean he wasn't possessive. He wanted to claim her for his own with every fiber of his being.

His room was the first on the left. He pushed the door open and took her in, his hand still wrapped around her upper arm. He didn't know why he was keeping such a tight hold on her. It wasn't as if she was going anywhere. It felt good to hold her though.

Once he had her safely alone in his room, he released her and pointed toward an open door situated to the right.

"Take a shower."

"Oh. Yes. Please," she said, brightening. "This has an en suite?"

"Uh huh. All the rooms do."

"This is a really nice safe house," she said, making casual conversation in an adorably awkward way. The blush on her cheeks told him she had no idea how to be around him after what she'd just done—and what he'd just seen done to her. "You've all got your own rooms and en suites and everything."

He wasn't really listening. He was watching her as she stepped into the bathroom.

"Leave the door open."

She looked over her shoulder with a curious glance.

"I want to see you."

She hesitated, but left the door open.

"Good girl."

Lacey gave him a nervous smile. "I guess I should get used to this."

"Probably," Chase agreed. This was the first chance they'd really had to talk since she'd called him in a panic. It was a more stilted conversation than he'd imagined, but then again, nothing about the day had gone as he'd predicted.

"This is nice," she said, looking around the small bathroom. It was alright. It wasn't much, a shower and a basin and a toilet. Everything a man needed. And now everything she needed. "You have a towel?"

She'd just been held down and fucked in two of her sweet holes. She was naked from the waist down. He could see the sheen of cum and pussy juice on her thighs. Ravaged. The word thrust itself into his head.

"You don't seem to object to any of this," he noted. "And yeah, I've got towels."

"I should be dead, Chase," she said, stripping her top off over her head. "I've been held captive and tortured before. I've..." She trailed off. "What Rex and Max did hardly registers."

He was simultaneously glad and sad. Glad that she was actually handling this situation, so far at least. Sad that she'd been conditioned to think that being held as the sex toy for five men who could trade her back and forth wasn't so bad.

She turned the shower on and cast a little smile at him. "Were you expecting me to beg for mercy or something, Chase? I know I don't deserve it."

Fuck. He felt his heart crack. He was feeling more sorry for her than she was for herself. He stood there, arms folded over his chest as she got into the shower. Then he went and leaned against the frame of the bathroom door, watching as the water flowed over her body. She had a nice figure, full ass and thighs, feminine curves top and bottom. Everything where it should be. She took care of herself, physically at least.

"So what are you going to do to me?" She asked the question as she tossed her head back, letting the water pull her long dark hair away from her face in a beautiful cascade.

"I'm going to talk to you."

"Talk?" She pulled her head back in surprise. "Twenty grand is a lot of talk, Chase."

"I don't care about the money."

It was true. He didn't. He also didn't care about merely fucking her. He wanted to know her. Traditional maybe, but that's the kind of guy he was.

"You're sweet," she said, flashing him a smile.

Sweet? Maybe. Cautious, definitely. Especially when it

came to her. Lacey had been on his mind for a long time. Now he had her, he wasn't in any rush. Even if Max and Rex were. Even if she was. They were still essentially strangers.

"You have no idea how good it feels to take a shower and not be scared that someone's going to come for me," she said, lathering soap over her skin. "It's been a while since I got to feel safe."

He allowed himself a smile. She felt safe with them. In spite of the fact that she'd spent the day being abducted and fucked, she trusted them to keep her alive—and do a lot more besides.

This was more complicated than he wanted it to be. If they'd met under other circumstances, he could see himself dating someone like Lacey, but neither of their lives were conducive to dating. So this was it. This was how it was happening.

"I'm going to need the morning-after pill," she said as she turned the shower off. "Rex might not care about birth control, but I'm not having a baby while the government wants me dead."

She was so matter of fact about it. It almost made him sad.

"You and Rex. Are you okay after…"

"Yeah," she said with an embarrassed smile. "I probably shouldn't be, but… I don't know. I…"

She looked down at her toes as Chase wrapped a towel around her. "It's alright to enjoy it," he murmured in her ear. "It doesn't make you a bad person."

"It doesn't make me any worse than what you already think I am," she said with a little shrug as she pulled away from him. He let her go. This situation was complicated in so many ways and it had escalated in a matter of hours in a completely unpredictable way. A concrete assassination attempt, Rex's declaration of ownership, everything. It was a lot for him. And if it was lot for him, he knew it was probably too much for her.

"Well, there's one thing you don't need to worry about. Rex had a vasectomy years ago."

"Oh. Okay. Cool. Then I'm gonna need an STD panel."

"We're clean," Chase reassured her. "We take regular tests."

"Because of the gangbangs you regularly have?" She gave him a cheeky little grin.

"Because we got into the habit early on when we were still in the military. Doesn't work if someone's dripping from their dick during a mission."

"Well, I'm clean," she said. "I haven't had sex since… well, a while. And I got tested after Venezuela. Several times."

He winced internally at what must have been the reason for that.

"You know what happened to us after Venezuela, but we never talked about what happened to you. Not about what happened there, or what happened since."

"I don't talk about what happened there," she said. Her dark hair had a slight wave now that it was wet. It hung forward over her head as she lowered it. "It's best not to."

He felt a tightening in his chest, an anger that had to be restrained. "Okay," he said. "Get dried off and get into bed."

"Yessir," she beamed with an arch little wink—perhaps a little too arch.

She probably thought he was intending on having sex with her. The truth was she'd already been fucked enough for one day. He wanted her in bed because he didn't have any clothes for her and he wanted her to be warm. While she did as she was told, snuggling underneath the covers, he went to the kitchen.

She needed food. He needed food. It had been a long, stressful day and the basics needed to be dealt with. Chase got started fixing something to eat, putting a pot of water on to boil.

"What are you doing?" Col perked up from the couch.

"Making food."

Col scowled. "You've left her alone? She could run away!"

"We have sensors that tell us if a fly farts," Chase said. "She's butt naked in bed. She's not going anywhere. Besides, what do you care, Col? It'd make your life easier if she did run off into the woods."

"I don't want more trouble," Col growled. "She should stay in the cage."

"Leave him, Col," Rex drawled.

Col went away muttering, leaving Chase to fix dinner. It was a welcome respite. He liked Col. Col was a brother to him, but when the guy got a hair up his ass he was relentless. It was an incredible quality to have in the field, but in interpersonal relationships it could make him a nightmare.

"You should at least be getting your money's worth," Col added as he slumped back in front of the television.

Chase ignored the comment. There was no rush to have sex. He had no intention of letting Lacey get away from him again. She'd been on his mind from the moment they rescued her, and having her back in his world, let alone in his bed, was enough for now.

When he was done fixing some pasta, he put two bowls on a tray and carried it into the bedroom.

Lacey was still in bed. Hadn't moved an inch. It wasn't any incredible act of obedience. It was because she was fast asleep, curled up beneath his blankets. Adorable. She was so small in so many ways, and yet everywhere she went, chaos erupted. She needed to be protected. She needed to be kept under control. He was looking forward to doing both.

Chase carried the tray back out to the living room. He'd made enough for everybody to eat, so he walked into a room of slurping, except for Brian who liked to cut his pasta before he ate it.

"Back already?" Rex lifted his head from his food. "Didn't think we'd see you until late tomorrow."

"She's asleep."

55

Col rolled his eyes. "You're going to pay twenty grand to let her sleep?"

"Yeah, I am."

"Idiot," Col snorted.

"Col, leave it!" Rex interjected.

Chase had about had enough of Col's attitude. He sat down in an armchair a few feet away from the couch where Col was sitting and took an aggressive bite of his meal before engaging the man. "You think we're just going to fuck her every minute of every day for forever?"

"No. I think you idiots are going to get your dicks wet and then she's going to fuck you all a hundred times harder than you could ever fuck her. And I think I'm the moron who knows better than to trust someone who already gave her word once and didn't keep it." Col slammed his bowl down on the coffee table.

Chase sat back, struck silent. Col had a good point. A really good point—one he couldn't rebut. Lacey hadn't exactly been trustworthy in her limited dealings with them. The past was one thing, but the present was also a concern. If she wrote another one of her tell-alls, the consequences could be even more dire. But, at the end of the day, trustworthy or not, she was in need. Her fate seemed to be connected to theirs. And he'd rather she was alive than dead.

"Now she's asleep, can we talk about the real reason we're doing this?" Brian finished eating and grabbed his computer.

"The real reason?" Chase was confused.

"The data she has," Rex clarified. "We have a buyer."

"What?" Chase narrowed his eyes. The hair on the back of his neck and arms was rising as he realized there was yet another layer to this shit show.

"The information she has is worth something. A lot of something," Rex explained. "She owes us. Now she gets to pay us back."

"Coming in her pussy wasn't enough?"

"Not even close," Rex said. "Don't act like she's a sweet

innocent little girl. She's basically a spy."

"She's a journalist."

"A journalist with information on a high-ranking senator. A journalist with a payload she isn't going to get to cash in on without our help."

Chase felt his mood shift darkly. "You didn't say a word about this when you agreed to help. The sex is one thing, but this is…"

"You got us on board by telling us she was in trouble because of information she held." Rex leaned forward, his hands clasped together. "Did you really think we wouldn't be interested in what she had? Did you think we'd drop everything to help someone who destroyed our lives for no return?"

"No pussy is that good, Chase." It was Col who spoke again. Chase was getting ever closer to decking him.

"Col, shut up," Rex snapped, standing up to take control of the situation. He stood over Chase in a way Chase didn't really entirely care for. It was a domineering pose, not so subtly reminding everybody who was ultimately in charge.

"I get you feel a little blindsided, but you brought us in on this today. We've had some time to think, and Brian's had time to get a handle on what she might have. He thinks it's worth something."

"Whatever it is, she's probably not going to give it to us," Chase said.

"She doesn't have a choice."

Chase looked at his comrades with a stony expression. Nothing about this felt right. Taking her as their own had been pushing it, but she'd agreed, at least partially. This? He didn't know Lacey very well, but he knew her work was her life. It had almost claimed her life on several occasions. He had a feeling she was more ready to sleep with them than she was to share her research—especially if they were going to sell it.

The conversation was interrupted abruptly with a high-pitched scream. It was the cry of a woman in absolute terror.

The sound zipped through Chase, throwing him from the chair in an instant. The others were close behind him. They all ran to Chase's room to find Lacey sitting bolt upright in bed, still screaming, her face fraught with terror.

"Shit."

Chase pulled her into his arms, but she didn't wake up. She was caught in some desperate state between sleep and awareness, the dark space where nightmares reigned. They were all familiar with it to one extent or another. This was par for the course with anyone whose life was one long traumatic situation.

"Don't kill me!" She pushed against him, her arms flailing wildly.

She was staring at something none of them could see, some monster her mind had manufactured.

Chase kept a hold of her anyway, running his hand over her hair, making soft soothing noises until she started to quieten a little. Her screams turned to soft whimpers, though she was still no more awake than she had been when they came in.

"Great. So she's a slut and she's crazy." Col muttered the words, or something like them under his breath. Chase didn't really hear them properly, but Max apparently did. He spun on his heel and punched Col. Hard. The satisfying crunch of fist against nose woke Lacey up with an even louder scream. Chase had to grab on to her to stop her from basically exploding across the room in a panic.

"You saw what she looked like when we found her. You saw how it was. What she went through," Max thundered at Col, displaying very rare anger. "Don't talk shit about her."

"Fuck you, idiot. Stick your dick in her and fall in love," Col spat, storming from the room, his nose pouring with blood.

"Out!" Rex thundered. "Everybody out *now*!"

"I'm staying," Max insisted.

"Fine, everybody else out. Col, go to the damn bathroom and I'll set your nose."

CHAPTER TEN

Lacey

She was surrounded by men, some of them swearing and cursing. For a second she didn't recognize any of them. She was back in Venezuela. She was captive. She was going to be killed. This was it. It was happening.

"Shhhh. It's okay…"

She blinked and saw Chase next to her. Chase. Oh, thank god. He could help her. Save her. She grabbed him, opening her mouth to tell him that he needed to help her, but nothing came out. She was suddenly vocally paralyzed. The more she tried to yell the less anything came, but her throat was raw as if she had been screaming for hours. Finally, a thin cry escaped her, incoherent and pathetic.

"Get her something to drink, Max. Something hot."

Max. The name sank into her consciousness and then she remembered. Three years rushed back in a tidal wave of time to the present moment. Now she knew where she was. Not Venezuela. America. She was safe, or at least as safe as it was possible for her to ever be.

"I'm sorry," she said softly, realizing that she'd just made a huge fool of herself.

"Don't be sorry. You've got nothing to be sorry for."

"I've got a lot to be sorry for," she said, her eyes welling with tears, which she blinked back quickly as she tried to get herself under control. She did not like being weak or vulnerable. She liked being tough. Whatever life threw at her, she could take it. That was fine when she was awake, but when she fell asleep the demons found her in the dark and took advantage.

"Not for having a nightmare," he said, his voice rumbling through her. "How often do they happen?"

Lacey was reluctant to talk about the situation. She'd never told anyone about the nightmares. Just slept with the lights on and sometimes had a stuffed animal with her. A big stuffed dog named Furdinand who had been left behind in her apartment.

"Lacey," Chase prompted. "I need to know."

"Do you? Why?"

"Because we're looking after you, and that means taking care of your needs and not letting you scream all night. Tell me," he insisted. "How often and how bad are they?"

She bit her lower lip, then figured there was no real harm in telling him. He'd already seen her in the embarrassing state.

"It happened a lot after Venezuela and then less for a while, and then all this stuff happened, and… it's worse when I'm stressed."

"Yeah," he nodded. "That makes sense. Okay. You have meds for it?"

"No," she scowled. "It's fine. Like I said, I don't usually get them unless someone tries to kill me, and then a bunch of men kidnap me and ravish me."

"Have you seen someone about it, like a therapist?"

"I'm therapy resistant," she said ruefully.

"You mean you're a pain in the ass," Chase smiled, pressing a tender kiss to her forehead. "I've got you. You're safe."

She felt safe. She felt about the safest she had ever felt

in her life. The night terrors made her so physically afraid she could barely breathe, so the contrast of waking in his arms was incredible. She was held. Hard male flesh was wrapped around her, protecting her. She rested her head against Chase's shoulder and breathed deeply.

"Chase!" Max called out.

"Yeah?"

"I don't know how to make hot chocolate!"

Chase snorted. "Come on," he said. "Wear the blanket. I'll make you something to drink."

Lacey shuffled out with Chase, the quilt wrapped around her nice and snugly. Still half asleep, she stood in the kitchen as Chase started to heat some milk for her. This would be such a nice little domestic moment if it were just the two of them. But it wasn't just the two of them. The other men were somewhere toward the bathroom, making noises at one another. The door must have been open, because she could hear the conversation quite clearly.

"Ow, fuck!" Col's voice sounded pained and nasal.

"Quit whining," Rex ordered. "And hold still."

Curious as ever, Lacey shuffled toward the bathroom, hoping to catch a glimpse of what was going on. As she shuffled into line of sight she saw that Col was standing in the middle of the floor, his shirt covered in blood. Rex was in front of him. He had a towel in his hand and he was reaching for Col's nose.

Lacey shut her eyes, sensing the next part was going to be gross. There was a crunch and a click and a curse as Rex reset Col's nose. He was going to be wearing a hell of a bruise for a long time, probably two black eyes.

"Lacey, get back over here," Chase called out, noticing that she'd wandered away.

She obeyed, walking back to the kitchen just brimming with questions. "What happened to him?"

"Max hit him," Chase said, mixing warm milk and chocolate powder.

"Why?"

"Don't worry about that," Chase said, handing her a mug of hot chocolate. It smelled delicious and she allowed herself to be distracted by it as she leaned against the kitchen counter and sipped at it, her gaze firmly locked across the room where Col and Rex were emerging, Col still cursing up a storm.

"Where the fuck is Max?"

"Here." Max lumbered out of the hallway. "You got something to say to me?"

"You bet I fucking do," Col hissed. "This is a mistake. You're all making a huge mistake because none of you can see past your own dicks."

"Col, that's enough…" Rex started to say, but Col wasn't listening. Lacey huddled closer to Chase as Col launched into a tirade.

"You're all fucking stupid if you think she won't sell us out. You think the nation won't want a follow-up where the reporter who broke the Venezuela story gets abducted and fucked for money? You think she's not making little notes in her head right fucking now? You think she's not finding a new way to describe us? You want to be a *grizzled wolf* again, Rex? Or an *all-American superhero*, Chase? Fucking stupid."

He was quoting her article practically verbatim. She had taken some poetic license when describing her rescuers years earlier. Hearing the words snarled at full volume made her blush with embarrassment and anger.

"I'm not going to write a story about you," she said, speaking up for herself.

"We've heard that before."

"Yeah, well. I learned my lesson," she said, trembling as she tried to defend what was basically indefensible. Col had no reason to trust her, no matter what she said. "I'm not going to be a journalist anymore. I'm done. I'm going to burn the information I have and…"

"Whoa there," Rex interjected. "Let's not be hasty here. Why don't you give us the information for safekeeping?"

"Rex…" Chase started to speak, but Rex cut him off with a dark look, as if there was something he really didn't want said, especially not in front of her.

"No," Lacey insisted. "I'm going to destroy the evidence, and I'm going to give the people who are after me proof that I destroyed it, and then maybe they'll leave me alone and maybe you can believe that I'm really done breaking stories. I can delete the files easily. Brian, can I borrow your laptop?"

Brian was sitting in the corner of the room and had been conspicuously staying out of the drama, but the moment she asked to use his laptop, he looked up with an expression that was slightly more horrified than it would have been if she'd asked to fuck his mother.

"Nobody touches my computer except me. You can give me the password and the file location and I'll destroy it for you."

She bit her lower lip. "Okay."

"Lacey…" Chase tried to interject again.

"That's enough, Chase," Rex said grimly. "Brian, take Lacey to your room and get what needs to be done out of the way."

CHAPTER ELEVEN

Rex

"I'm not going to let you use her," Chase hissed. "Not this way. Sex is one thing, but this is a betrayal. Plain and simple."

Rex calmed himself inwardly as he prepared to deal with this latest tantrum. Chase was an idealist. Always had been. He wanted to be the good guy even when the 'good guy' was just a naive cartoon. It had been a lot easier when they were in the military and orders were orders. Nobody questioned him then. Now they had a lot more leeway for pushback.

"We're already using her," Rex said. "Besides, the information she has is information several other people died collecting. It means something. It shouldn't be deleted just because she loses her nerve."

"It means a payment to your bank account," Chase pointed out.

"It means a payment to all our bank accounts. It means Lacey gets to live. You think the people who are after her are just going to shake her hand and say thanks for deleting their data? No. They're cleaning up. They'll take her out with the rest of the trash. We're doing what's best for her."

Chase lifted his chin in a way that did not bode well. "You're lying to her, and I won't do that."

"Yes, you will," Rex said, his voice hard and steely. "You'll do it because I'm damn well ordering you to, and because it's what's best for all of us."

"You could just tell her…"

"And then I'd have to have two irritating conversations with mouthy subordinates instead of just one." Rex could hear the strain in his own voice. The brutal part of him, the part he kept well in check, was crying out to lay a beating on these whelps who dared question him.

Chase ground his teeth and glared at him with a mutinous gaze, but Rex knew damn well Chase would follow orders when it came down to it.

"You wanted our help on this." Rex softened his voice with some effort. "It comes at a price."

"And that price is using her sexually and then lying to her."

"Still better than her being tortured and killed, no? She's made no objections to our arrangement. I think she likes it. She's exactly the sort of girl who enjoys being used by men."

Chase clenched his fists. The threat of violence was in the air between them. Rex knew he should be de-escalating this, but there was no way to do that without being bluntly honest.

"She's no pure princess, Chase. She's a dirty little slut at heart. Nothing wrong with that. Nothing wrong with using a girl as nature intended."

"One more fucking word…" Chase growled.

"And what? You're going to break my nose too? Shall we all just break each other's noses over her?" Rex's voice was borderline mocking. "I know this doesn't suit you, Chase. I know you'd prefer to play house with her, but we don't have that luxury, and you know what else? She'd eat you alive if you tried."

"What do you mean?" Chase looked more confused

than angry.

"I mean she might seem small and scared now, but that girl in there is not an innocent little sweetheart. She's got a soul like steel. Think about where we met her, Chase. She didn't end up in a militia prison because she took a wrong turn in Caracas. She had been running with criminals for months before we got there. And now she's mixed up in some serious political shit. There's a trail of bodies, but she's still alive. Don't underestimate her just because she looks like Holly Homemaker. The truth is she's a buck twenty of trouble, tits, and ass. The sooner you realize that, the better."

Chase opened his mouth to reply, but before he could, Brian and Lacey could be heard returning. The conversation ended abruptly as Lacey entered the room at a fast shuffle, kicking the blanket out with her feet at every step. Brian followed behind her, his laptop clenched to his chest, both his arms wrapped around it.

Rex watched Chase melt when he looked at her. Goddamn. The boy had learned nothing.

"Done," she beamed, sidling up to Chase, wrapping her arms around his waist. "I feel so much better knowing that's gone."

Rex looked at Brian, who gave him a subtle thumbs-up behind her back. Good. It had been done quickly and smoothly and without her knowledge. She could stay blissfully unaware now. It wasn't really a betrayal. They'd keep their part of the deal. They'd keep her safe. It would probably mean keeping her close for the next few years, but Rex didn't see that as a hardship, more of a bonus—or a good deed. The world needed to be kept safe from the likes of Lacey.

She was snuggling into Chase like a happy kitten, looking up under her lashes at him. They were so damn enamored of each other. Rex didn't like that. At all. He hoped Chase wouldn't become a problem. Even Col was less of a concern than Chase at this point. Col might hate her guts, but he wasn't going to spill anything to her that she shouldn't hear.

"Let's go to bed," Chase murmured to Lacey.

Rex watched, his arms folded over his chest as they walked away together, looking like they were already a close couple. It hadn't even been six hours since he'd seen her for what was supposed to be the first time in three years and they already looked like they were about to head down the aisle together.

"Chase is going to fuck us," Col muttered, picking up Rex's thoughts. "Probably before he fucks her."

"Shut up already," Max interjected. "You're being a real asshole. What's wrong with you?"

"What's wrong with *you*?" Col began the bickering again.

"Okay, that's enough," Rex said, turning toward them. "Col, if you don't want to be part of this, you can leave. It will be harder without you, but you don't have to stay."

"So I lose my job and my family over that little b—"

"Don't," Rex interrupted him sharply. "Enough. We'll call you in as a contractor on jobs if you want, but you can't stay here and second guess my decisions. That's not how this works."

Col was a good man and truth be told, they couldn't really spare him. There was no excess fat in their unit. Everybody had a role to play and doing their work without Col would be stretching their resources a little too thin for Rex's liking, but having someone bitching and moaning the whole time wasn't going to help either.

"You don't have to like her," he continued. "But you do have to treat her with respect."

Col looked around. Rex could see he was trying to weigh up his support. He didn't have much. Max was firmly Team Lacey. The only possible convert was Brian, and he was back on his computer so intently he probably hadn't heard a word any of them had said.

"Fine," Col relented. "But I'm not sleeping with her."

"I'm sure she'll survive," Rex rumbled.

"I'm going out to the workshop," Brian declared. "I'll

see you guys in the morning."

He got up and walked out, laptop under his arm. That left Rex, Col, and Max alone in what was starting to feel like a depressing aftermath.

"We've all had a long day," Rex said. "Let's get some rest. Tomorrow we can start working on the information she has. You're going to get your payoff, Col. We're not doing this for nothing. Remember that."

CHAPTER TWELVE

Lacey

Lacey woke up wound in the arms of a strong man. For a brief moment of morning amnesia, she wasn't sure exactly where she was, or who she was with, but she knew she felt good. One brawny arm was wrapped around her waist, and something nice and thick was poking her in the rear. She rolled over slowly and looked into the face of the man she had been dreaming about for three years.

Chase. She couldn't believe she was really in bed with him. A little sexual ache between her thighs reminded her that she had broken her dry spell. But not with him. With another man. God. What was she doing? Her clit tingled at the memory of being held down and fucked by Rex.

Now she wanted Chase. Her pussy was sensitive and a little sore, but feeling his morning erection against her thigh was too much temptation. She reached down and wrapped her fingers around his cock, slowly stroking the shaft.

He stirred a little, his cock twitching in her hand. Lacey stroked him gently, reflecting on the events that had brought her here to him—and to the four other men, each of whom had claim to her under the terms she had agreed to. It was a potentially dangerous arrangement, and in the light of a new day, that only made it all the more alluring.

Lacey would never have admitted it, but danger excited her. She could have quit journalism after Venezuela. She could have come home and gotten some local beat and never covered anything more exciting than a county fair. Instead, she'd gone to the very heart of power and corruption and stuck her nose in until someone tried to bite it off.

Now she was at the mercy of five virile men. Men who took what they wanted. Men who wanted her. In the privacy of her own mind, she allowed herself to revel in the deliciousness of it.

Lacey had never once managed a traditional relationship. Most men couldn't keep up with her. They got tired of her being out all hours, being buried in her work, the frequent visits from unsavory characters. Cops and criminals alike, Lacey had connections everywhere. She'd tried dating throughout the spectrum, but it never worked out and she'd been single for the last year, when she realized that it was starting to get dangerous not just for her, but for anyone too close to her.

These men weren't like other men. They were stronger. They seemed to understand her better than almost anyone else, each in different ways. Even Col knew her in some way. He hated her, but she didn't really blame him for that. She was more surprised the others didn't.

"What do you think you're doing, my girl?"

Chase's sleepy morning rumble startled her out of her thoughts. Her hand stilled on his cock.

"Uhm…" She looked at him under her lashes. "Touching you?"

"Not now, Lacey," he said, gently unfurling her fingers from his rod.

"Not now? When?" She hated sounding pouty.

"When it's right," he said cryptically.

"It feels right to me." She gave him her sexiest smile, the

one that usually got marks to spill all the info she needed. Chase just frowned.

"Lacey, if you keep tempting me, I am going to turn you over my knee and spank your butt red."

She let out a little giggle. "Oh, really?"

His brow rose and his pupils narrowed just a little. "I'm not joking."

"Uh huh…" She reached back and pushed the blankets off her naked butt, rolling her hips to make her cheeks gyrate alluringly. "You're going to spank me just because I want you… ow!"

He'd reached out and swatted her butt hard enough to make her hips sink back down to the bed, and to impart a serious sting to her rear.

"Ow, Chase!" She didn't have to pretend to pout now.

"I warned you."

"Yeah, but I didn't expect you to actually do that. I thought you were the nice one."

"I am the nice one," Chase winked. "That's why you got one warning slap and not a full on thrashing."

"Lucky me," she grumbled, turning around so he couldn't reach her rear so easily anymore. That left her naked body exposed to Chase completely. She wanted him. Of all the men, she wanted him the most. But he didn't seem interested in her. He looked at her with appreciation, but not with unchained lust. There was something else between them, something she didn't understand at all. In the absence of explanation, she took it as rejection.

"Fine," she said. "If you don't want me, someone else will."

She got out of bed and stamped down the hall to the kitchen before Chase could get up and stop her.

Rex was up, getting some coffee. It struck her again just how hot he looked with the salt and pepper five-o'clock shadow around his chin and jaw. He was also just barely dressed, wearing striped blue pajama pants and nothing else. His torso was hard and well proportioned. He had the body of an active duty soldier, all practical working muscle.

"What the hell are you doing?" He asked the question when he saw her standing there utterly naked.

"Chase won't fuck me."

"Lacey..." Chase followed her in.

"No. I want to have sex," she said. "So if you won't... eeeeep!"

Her squeal was caused by being grabbed, carried across the room, and pushed over the back of the couch. In seconds her bare pussy was raised and on display. She felt the head of Rex's cock against her entrance. Unlike Chase, he wasted no time at all in fulfilling her request.

"You want to be fucked, is that it?"

"Yes, Daddy."

She felt him hesitate at the word, then a second later, he drove inside her. Deep. One long thrust inside her pussy that filled her all the way to her cervix. She didn't know why she'd called him that. He was in no way like her father. It was just an impulse that had taken her when she felt his energy. Rex was more than dominant. He was the emotional center of the group, the maker of rules. He was the one who decided everything, and as she laid there, her ass in the air, her pussy wrapped around his cock, she felt a kind of inexplicable erotic peace filling her up along with his dick. This was how things were meant to be. This was how she was meant to wake up.

"Bad girl," Rex lectured, holding himself still inside her. "You want to make Chase jealous by having me take your pussy?"

"Maybe..." She squeaked the word as her tight hole tried to accommodate him.

"I don't think that's going to work out for you," Rex said, pulling all the way out, then pushing his cock all the way back inside her in one languid stroke. "Chase isn't jealous of what I do to your pussy. Are you, Chase?"

"Not at all," Chase said, looking at her with a bemused expression. "Especially not when she calls you Daddy."

"You're exactly the sort of girl who needs a daddy to fuck her, aren't you, Lacey?"

"Yes, sir," she mumbled, embarrassment flowing through her veins. She needed this. She needed sex to wipe away the stress.

"You've got a daddy now," he growled. "You've got a daddy who will fuck your pussy long and hard, who will spank your little ass when you need it. You've got a daddy you're going to have to obey."

Lacey moaned as she was fucked long and hard, Rex's cock making her pussy stretch and grip with every one of his thrusts. Rex understood what she needed, and he didn't hold back. He used her until... ping! A metallic sound across the room intervened.

"That's my toast," he said, pulling out. "Chase, you can take over if you like…"

"Please," she whimpered. "Don't stop…"

"Breakfast is the most important meal of the day," Rex said, slapping her ass.

"Chase…"

Chase shook his head. "I don't know, Lacey, I don't know that you deserve my cock after that tantrum."

She pouted and started to stand up.

"No," he said quickly. "Stay there. Just like that."

"Why? You don't want me."

"Oh, I want you," he said, his eyes gleaming with lust. She could see the hard line of his erection underneath his boxers. "But you need to learn a lesson. You don't demand anything from me, girl. Including sex."

"What's for breakfast?" Max asked the question as he pushed his way into the room, dressed in jeans and a football jersey. He stopped dead seeing Lacey bent over the couch, her half-fucked pussy on display.

"She is," Chase said with a smirk. "Mouthy girl wanted to be fucked."

"Is that right?" Max smirked back. "Goddamn, Chase. This was the best idea you ever had." He slapped Chase on the back and walked around behind Lacey.

Lacey held on to the couch as the second cock of the day sank inside her. This was fucked up. This was wrong. This was hot as hell. Max reached forward, took her by the shoulders and rammed his cock deep into her already warmed-up pussy, stroking in and out with rolling motions of his hips that made her sex melt around him.

Brian was up next. He fixed himself some cereal, his gaze settling on her as Max kept publicly fucking her, making good use of her pussy.

She was the center of their attention, Chase, Rex, Brian, and Max all fixated on her, in between sips of coffee and bites of toast, anyway. There was something hot and twisted about how casually they were using her, as if fucking a naked girl over the couch, sharing her wet pussy between their hard cocks was just totally natural.

"Don't come in her," Rex cautioned. "Not without protection."

"Of course," Max snorted, his cock throbbing deep in her pussy. "Wouldn't want to knock her slutty little cunt up."

Lacey let out a moan of embarrassed arousal. Every thrust was making her clit grind against the arm of the couch, pushing her toward an orgasm that was not all that far away and hadn't been since Rex had picked her up and manhandled her into the fucking position.

Max stroked inside her a few more times, then pulled out and she felt his cum spraying all over her ass, hot spurts of it coating her cheeks, missing the wet slit of her pussy entirely. She was left without orgasm and somehow disappointed. Her inner walls clenched as she looked hopefully at Chase and Brian. She had already given up all semblance of modesty or chastity. That had been ripped away by Rex last night. Now what she wanted was release, to have a hot load of her protectors' seed inside her.

"Please…" she whimpered to Chase. "Please, sir…"

"Oh, sir," Rex noted. "She's getting more polite."

"Mhm, she is," Chase agreed. "Almost like she knows how to behave herself after all."

"I need to come," she whimpered, glancing hopefully over at Brian. He was watching her, but she didn't think he was going to come over and fuck her. He didn't seem like the type to bang a girl in front of his boss and colleagues, but she got her hopes up when he opened his mouth to speak.

"Does someone want to help me bring something inside? It's too heavy for one person." Brian's all too pedestrian comment dashed her hopes. She'd been fucked twice, but not allowed to come. It wasn't fair.

"You stay there," Chase insisted. "Everyone hasn't had their turn yet."

"You're being mean," she whimpered.

"No, I'm being nice," he smiled. "I'm making sure you get everything you wanted."

"Anyone?" Brian spoke up again.

"I will," Max said. "Keep your hair on, little guy."

Lacey stayed dangling over the couch, wondering what was in store for her next. They couldn't just leave her here all day, surely, just coming by occasionally to give her pussy a casual fuck. The thought made her tingle. They could do exactly that and so much more. She'd given herself to them without reserve.

Max and Brian soon came back in with a bunch of pieces of metal and pneumatics and a battery and a rubber dildo. Lacey looked on, at first with interest, and then with a growing sense of horror as Brian fitted the pieces together to form a long shaft attached to a rotating motor. The dildo was affixed to the shaft in very short order. He stood back with a proud smile and let them all see what he had been up to.

"Sick little fucker," Rex chuckled. "Too lazy to fuck her yourself?"

"This is more efficient," Brian smiled. He turned and crooked his finger at Lacey. "Come here."

Brian didn't have an uber-dominant persona, but he didn't need one. There was a charming force of will that made her want to obey him, though she glanced at Chase first to make sure he wouldn't object to her getting up from the couch. He nodded briefly and so she got up and made her way over and around to where Brian was standing. Looking at him, she felt herself blush. He had a unique kind of attractiveness in the group, an elegance that made her feel her crude nudity more than before.

If he was judging her in any way, he didn't show it. When she reached him, Brian took her by the hand like a gentleman and had her kneel down on hands and knees. Having assumed the position, she heard him tut quietly, then felt him take a cloth and wipe her rear off, removing Max's cum.

She was nervous as Brian adjusted the mechanical cock at her pussy, the cool, lifeless pseudo-flesh thick and firm against her swollen lower lips. She heard a click and then a hum, and then the dildo surged forward, parting her pussy and sliding about three inches deep.

"Oh, fuck!" she gasped.

"Looks good," he mused, retracting the shaft and squirting a little lube onto the toy. "I think we're ready right out of the box! That almost never happens."

He adjusted it a little more, tinkering around a bit before setting the toy into constant motion, not too fast, not too slow, a steady series of strokes that forced the dildo a little deeper every time until he set the calibration at a decent six inches inside her. She knew that because he announced it to the group, almost more pleased with his own technical prowess than with the eroticism of the moment.

It wasn't anything like being taken by a man. The machine moved backward and forward in clean, straight, repetitive strokes that stimulated her pussy in a whole new way. It felt incredible, perhaps because it was designed only for her pleasure. She didn't have to worry about the dildo's experience. All that mattered was her, her pussy being filled, pounded, stretched.

Brian stood proudly next to her as she moaned and writhed, the dildo making obscene wet sounds as it slid in and out of her sex.

"We can use this as often as we need to," he said, speaking to the others more than to her. "And we can have different attachments, one for her ass as well as her pussy, a tickler for her clit. I could even adjust it for a spanking machine…"

"What the fuck is going on?"

Col's growl interrupted Brian's speech, but not the machine that kept squeaking away, shafting her pussy with steady strokes.

Through her desperate moans Lacey noticed that he looked like shit. His eyes were both black and puffy underneath as he stared at her and the sex machine.

"She's been here one day and we're making fuck toy contraptions?" He snorted. "Jesus."

"Brian's making them," Rex said. "He outsourced his cock."

Col made a grunting noise and poured himself some coffee.

"And I can turn it up," Brian said, twisting a dial held in his hand. Lacey let out a squeak as the frequency doubled, the dildo finding her pussy twice as fast, diving in and out of her wet lips over and over as she shook and moaned.

"It's too much!" She pulled off the toy cock, her thighs shaking as she collapsed onto the floor. It was so fucking intense and she hadn't even come yet. Just taking that level of stimulation had pushed her body into a state of arousal that made every muscle feel weak. Her pussy was on fire, her clit yearning for touch, but all she could do was kneel there for the moment and breathe deeply.

"Are you alright?" Brian crouched down next to her and pulled her hair away from her face so he could see her. She looked into his handsome face and nodded.

"Uhm mhm, it's just really intense…"

He smiled and she felt her stomach quiver. Goddamn. He was hot, and kind of twisted, which only made him more attractive in her eyes.

"I can slow it back down," he said. "Do you want to get back on?"

"No," Rex intervened. "I want back inside her."

Brian backed away and Lacey bit her lower lip but stayed in position as the older man approached her, knelt down behind her on the floor, and pushed his cock into her pussy without any ceremony at all. In seconds he had pushed her further down into a prone position and was fucking her against the carpet. She moaned, spreading her legs, her clit grinding against the floor as Rex slammed her pussy, his hot bare cock feeling a hundred times better than the sterile machine, which couldn't growl against the back of her neck, or reach beneath her and grab her breasts, pinching her nipples as he rode her to orgasm.

Rex did all those things and more, his sexual dominance complete as he fucked her roughly, her amply lubricated slit taking every primal thrust. All thoughts were driven from her head as she was taken there on the floor, her pussy put to hard use yet again. Somewhere in the midst of his erotic onslaught, she was finally triggered into release by the pulsing and throbbing that accompanied his orgasm.

"Ohhhh, my god! My god!" She gasped and moaned as she came violently beneath Rex, her pussy flooded with his cum for a second time. God, she hoped that vasectomy would hold. He thrust his seed deep inside her several times over, making sure her cunt was good and bathed in it before pulling out and standing up.

"M'lady," he said in mock gentlemanly tones as he bent down and offered her his hand to help her stand up. Lacey's legs were trembling as she got to her feet. Every hour with these men seemed to bring some new and even more intense sexual perversion. She leaned against Rex for a moment as she got her breath and strength back. She was covered in his cum again, his hot seed making her inner thighs sticky and messy. He had left her in a complete state of shameful sexual conquest. When she looked down she could see pressure marks from the carpet around her nipples where she'd been pushed with each of his rough thrusts. He'd used her and used her well, there was no doubt about that.

"So this is going to be it, huh. Sex until the bad people forget about me?"

"You wish," Rex said, slapping her bare ass. "You're going to work around here too. Go get some breakfast and clean up the dishes when you're done."

Breakfast. That actually sounded good. But she needed to clean herself up before she cleaned any dishes. She could smell his scent all over her, mingling with Max's musk.

She'd had two men and a machine before breakfast.

It was twisted. It was wrong. It was so fucking hot.

She excused herself to the bathroom and cleaned up a little, running a warm cloth across her ravaged pussy. It was sensitive to the touch. Sore, but not in a bad way. As she looked at herself in the mirror, Lacey wondered what was happening to her. If anyone had told her she'd willingly give herself to five men to just fuck her as they pleased, she would have… well, she probably would have tried to interview them for their no doubt bizarre story.

It's survival, she told herself. *You're doing this to live.*

But it was more than that. Rex hadn't forced anything. What he'd done was given her an excuse to be as open to sex as she was to life. In any other circumstances, allowing this many men access would have made her judge herself too harshly to enjoy any of it. She'd have been worried about being thought of as a slut. She would have been thinking how to spin it into her next exposé. She would never have been able to surrender to her own desires and just let these powerful, brutally smart men take her body as nature had intended it to be taken.

She'd once read there was evidence that ancient humans had reproduced in orgiastic styles. There was a book that posited that gangbangs were how nature had intended humans to be intimate. Something about penises being designed to scoop other semen out of the vagina they were fucking and embed their own as deeply as possible. She couldn't remember all the details, but right now she felt a flush of sexual satisfaction she had never felt after being with just one man. Maybe there was something to that author's theory.

Maybe... she smiled to herself. Maybe she could just regard all of this as research. And maybe, one day, a long time from now, she could tell the tale of what was being done to her without the guys all freaking out and feeling betrayed. Nobody could fire them now, after all.

"Good one," she muttered to herself. "You can't ruin their lives because you already ruined their lives."

Guilt made an unwelcome return. This sex was supposed to be a punishment. She knew that even though they hadn't exactly been punishing about it. If they wanted to hurt her, they could. There would be no stopping them.

"Satisfied?" Chase murmured the question in her ear as she went to the kitchen and made some toast for herself. He was behind her, his arms wrapped around her waist, the stubble around his chin grazing her shoulder and neck.

The answer was no. She wasn't satisfied because she had wanted *him*. Sex with Rex and Max was hot. The machine had been an interesting experience too, but there was something inside her that called to Chase, and he wasn't answering.

"Why won't you fuck me?"

"It hasn't even been a day," Chase reminded her. "I take my time. Does that make sense?"

She bit her lower lip. "Ordinarily, yeah. But when every dick in this domicile is coming for me except yours, it feels weird."

"I'm in this for more than my dick," Chase said, rubbing her shoulders. "You want a shirt or something?"

She'd kind of stopped noticing that she was naked. How

weird that she'd cleaned herself and not even bothered to try to put anything on.

"Um, yes, please," she said as a sudden blush made its way over her body and face. "Some clothes would be good."

"I'll get you a t-shirt," he said. "Keep you easy access."

She blushed and glanced in his direction. "Easy access for you?"

He smirked and swatted her butt. "Greedy girl," he murmured. "You've been fucked how many times this morning already?"

"Not enough, apparently."

"I don't think there's ever going to be an enough where you're concerned, Lacey," Chase smiled. "Get something to eat. I'll get you that shirt."

CHAPTER THIRTEEN

Chase

Jogging through the forest gave Chase a much needed chance to think. It also gave him a chance to hang with Col a bit. The last twenty-four hours had been pretty hard on them all in various ways, and though he and Col were on the opposite sides of the spectrum of opinion on Lacey, Col was still one of Chase's closest friends. They didn't have to agree on absolutely everything. Hell, after all they'd been through, they didn't have to agree on anything.

"So," Col said when they stopped to hydrate. "You do her yet?"

"No."

"Shit, why not?"

"Because it's too soon."

"Rex doesn't think so."

"Well, I'm not Rex," Chase said with a shrug.

"She's going to be stretched out by the time you get to her," Col teased. "Hotdog down a hallway. Especially with Brian's freaky machines."

"You're such an idiot," Chase snorted. "That is not how vaginas work."

"I don't get you," Col said. "I know you want her. Like, *want* her. And you're letting everyone else fuck her first? That doesn't make any sense at all."

"Fucking isn't everything," Chase said.

"Uhm… okay… no, but it's a lot." Col frowned. "You worried she's got something?"

"No," Chase said with a snort. "It's not that. It's…"

Col stood there silently, just looking at him. Chase knew from experience that Col wouldn't pry further, but he would listen if Chase wanted to tell him what was going on. And he did need to tell someone, because it was already feeling weird.

"I remember how she was in Venezuela. Every time I look at her I see…"

Col's expression hardened. "Yeah, I remember," he said. "They worked her the fuck over."

"Yes, they did," Chase agreed. "We didn't kill nearly enough of those bastards."

There was a silence of agreement in which they both stood with hard stares, each thinking of what they should have done. Chase couldn't get the sight of her out of his head. Lacey's hair was glossy now. Back then it had been frizzed and matted with her own blood. Her cute face had been misshapen with bruises, her lip fat and cut. There had been marks all over her body. And those were just the ones that they could see. The way she'd recoiled from him when he picked her up to get her out of there even though she was thrilled to be rescued told an unspoken story that made him furious to his very core.

"I wish we could have taken her with us instead of just dropping her in Caracas," Chase said. "She needed someone to stay with her, make sure she was alright."

"We didn't have a choice. We were under orders."

"I know, but I can't help thinking she wouldn't have fucked up as bad as she did if we'd just taken her."

"And if my uncle had tits he'd be my aunt," Col said sharply. "What's done is done. And you have to stop feeling sorry for her, or you're going to miss what you can get out of her."

"I'm not interested in what I can get out of her," Chase said. "I'm interested in a relationship. When everyone's done banging her, she's going to need someone to connect with. Someone who cares about her more than how hot and tight her holes are."

"So you're just going to let the rest of us do what we want to her until she falls for you?" Col laughed. "Chase, that is a shitty plan."

"Maybe," Chase admitted. Now that he said it out loud, it didn't make the most sense. "I'm kind of surprised how she's taken to all this. Most women wouldn't…"

"She's not most women."

That was true. Lacey wasn't most women. She wasn't most people, period. She was stunning. She was talented. She was brave. She was everything he wanted in a woman, but he couldn't bring himself to touch her because every time he looked at her, he saw the cowering victim she had been years ago. He wasn't the only one who cared about her either. Max's reaction to Col's stupid comment the night before showed that the protective urge ran through him as well.

"How's your face?" Chase changed the subject.

"Eh," Col shrugged. "It'll heal."

"You still pissed about her?"

"Yeah, but she's getting fucking railed," Col said. "I feel like we're getting our money's worth out of her, if nothing else."

It was true. Lacey was taking everything Rex and the others had to give her. She was holding up like a goddamn sexual champion. Chase wondered how long that would last.

CHAPTER FOURTEEN

Lacey
Five days later…

Life as the captive of an elusive mercenary force wasn't easy, but Lacey was starting to settle into it. Most nights she slept with Chase. He was easygoing about her sexual escapades with the other men, but he was absolutely insistent on having her in his bed. Every night she showered away the sweat and semen from other men and curled up in his arms and he cuddled her close and didn't have sex with her.

If he minded her being with the others, he kept it very well hidden. There was never so much as a flicker of jealousy that she could detect. His gaze was always appreciative, but also watchful. She was starting to think of him as her protector, a guardian angel in this group of lustful men who never seemed to tire of using her body, or seeing it taken.

Col had not broken his vow not to touch her either. He basically went about his business as if she wasn't there at all. It was almost worst being ignored than it had been being hated, though she knew she shouldn't really care what he thought.

Sometimes though, when he didn't know she was aware of him, she would catch him looking at her in a reflection. His expression wasn't angry or hateful; it was almost... wistful? That made no sense. Lacey tried not to read too much into it.

Really, she had only had sex with two of them so far. Max and Rex: the daddy and the laidback renegade of the group who didn't seem to care about anything other than the present. She liked Max very much. He was the most lighthearted of the group, and he kept her entertained with his antics.

"Wanna see me drink fire?" He popped up next to the porch one evening, a bottle of vodka in one hand and a lighter in the other. His grin was broad, his eyes lit with masculine mischief.

"Uhm, sure?"

"You can't drink fire," he said, his expression becoming serious. "Remember that."

"Oh. Okay."

"You can drink, or you can fire, but not at the same time. Alcohol is extremely flammable."

"Uh huh."

He'd obviously imbibed a fair amount of the bottle before giving her the PSA. He was slightly unsteady on his feet as he nodded in her direction. "And I'm not a Russian spy. It's just we only had vodka."

"I know you're not a Russian spy," Lacey smiled. "Because I'm a Russian spy!"

"Russian spy!" Max shouted. He leaped onto the balcony and began tickling her. Lacey slid from her chair, giggling and gasping for breath as his long fingers found all her most sensitive spots. Her shrieks and laughs soon brought Rex and Chase out onto the porch.

"What are you doing?" Rex demanded.

"I'm subduing this Russian spy," Max said, crouched over Lacey. "She's very very dangerink!"

"Go sober up," Rex sighed. "Lacey, get up and stop rolling on the floor."

"He started it," she said, brushing leaves from the shirt she was wearing. It belonged to Chase really. They still hadn't got her any clothes or underwear. She had washed what she was wearing when they took her and it was drying on an outside line, but in the meantime she just had long borrowed shirts and sweaters to keep her warm.

"Traitor," Max hissed. "Russian traitor spy!"

Lacey giggled as he reached out and gave her a big bear hug, picking her up off her feet entirely.

"Pretty spy," he added, cupping her ass before putting her back down.

Rex went back inside to his book. Chase stayed there, laughing as Max lowered her to the ground. Sometimes it was almost possible to forget that she was a captive. Sometimes she was just Lacey and these were just the men she happened to be staying in the forest with. Other times, she had to force herself from not mentally writing stories about them. Her mind was already thinking of ways she could describe Max—*a behemoth, gentle giant with a penchant for oral sex* came to mind.

"You should go inside," Chase said. "Dinner's almost ready and Brian wants you."

"He has prepared another dewice of erotik torment," Max said in his terrible Russian accent.

"I can't wait," Lacey grinned.

"You are a dewiant," Max declared, picking her up again. He carried her in through the door, squirming in his arms. "Brianski! I have you prisoner!"

"No!" Lacey pretended to try to wriggle away, only for Max to hold her all the more firmly. He carried her into the living room where Brian was setting up with machinery and ropes. "Help! I promise I'm not a spy!"

The words shot through her after leaving her lips. She'd screamed them before, and meant it. She hadn't ever imagined she'd be able to say anything like that again without shutting down completely, but with Max cradling her in his arms and Brian smiling at her with those wicked green eyes, she didn't shut down. She wasn't enveloped by panic. The past was retreating and being replaced with a much better present.

"I know you're scared of ropes," Brian said as Max settled her down on her knees in front of him. "But I'd like to tie you up tonight. It will make the machine work better."

He crouched down next to her, getting on her level, enveloping her with the warmth of his personality.

"It's okay," she smiled. "When you do it, it's different."

"Good," he said, his emerald gaze enchanting. "Take your shirt off."

She did as she was told, only breaking their gaze when it came over her head. He pulled it away from her and tossed it off to the side.

"You're beautiful, Lacey."

"Thank you," she blushed. Brian could be so sweet. His compliments were always gentle and considered. He was quite often removed from the group, locked in his own little world, but when he gave her his full attention he could sweep her off her feet.

He played the rope gently around her neck and let it slide down between her breasts. She let her breath out in a slow hiss as he let it slither over her skin, moving like a live thing in his expert hands. He had definitely done this before, and it was nothing like what it felt like when she'd been grabbed and bound previously. Every motion and touch was deliberate. He gave her instructions on how to position herself and she obeyed them, allowing him to wrap his rope around her, envelop her in his desire. He had her kneel down, her knees spread, her hands out in front of her, bound at the wrists and connected all the way back to her ankles so every motion made the ropes ride over her body, loops catching around her breasts and between her legs.

He was patient and methodical and slow, but before she knew it she was entirely captive to him and the machine was parting the petals of her sex.

"You're a good girl, Lacey," Brian praised her, his hand running down the length of her back in a soothing stroke. "This is going to be your reward."

She held her breath, and he turned the machine on. It began to slide into her slowly, the thick shaft of it working her inner walls with mechanical insistency and regularity.

"You're going to stay there," he said. "I'll feed you dinner here, you can watch television here. I want you here for hours."

"Hours?" She let out a little whimpered moan.

"Mhm." He stroked her hair away from her face. "All night long."

• • • • • • •

Three hours later…

Lacey was bound on the floor, her legs spread, her pussy wet and glistening and wrapped around the hard shaft of the machine, which Brian had set to slide in and out of her pussy just once a minute. Thirty seconds in, thirty seconds out. A slow fucking that was driving her mad with desire. He had kept his word, brought her food, fed her from his fingers as she crouched there like a captive animal, her sex taking every stroke the machine had for her with a greedy desire. It wasn't enough to come, but it was more than enough to send her into a state of pure arousal. Brian was the youngest of the men, but he knew what he was doing. Whenever she looked into his face with moaning need, he smiled that gentle knowing smile and reassured her she was doing well.

"I need more," she moaned. "Please, Brian…"

"You get to come a lot," he said. "Relax and enjoy the fucking, Lacey. Let your body be used. You don't need to orgasm tonight."

"But…"

"Shhhh…" He pressed a kiss to her forehead. "Let your

pussy take its punishment."

This was punishment. This was denial of what she needed more than anything in the world. Her body was flooded with pleasure hormones, endorphins making her feel floaty and peaceful—and so fucking horny she couldn't take it.

"We shouldn't have tied her up," Max said somewhere in her haze. "Then she could be getting us beers."

"Lazy girl, lying there being fucked," Rex drawled.

"She's just getting warmed up for our cocks," Max smirked.

"Not tonight," Chase said, spoiling the impending fun. "We've got an early start tomorrow. I'm taking Lacey to bed."

There was a round of groans, including from Lacey herself as Chase crouched down next to her and unbound her. Brian turned the machine off and slowly she slid off the dildo with a little moan. She hadn't come yet. She really, really needed to come. Brian really did know how to construct the most delicious positions of pure torment, and he'd left her in a truly desperate state.

Chase picked her up, knowing she wouldn't be steady on her feet. "Say goodnight to Brian."

"Goodnight to Brian," she mumbled, curling into Chase's body.

Her pussy was aching with desire and she pushed against him as he carried her back to the bedroom.

"Tonight," she whispered in his ear. "I need you tonight."

"You need to get some sleep," he said firmly, putting her down on the bed.

Lacey laid back and spread her legs, giving him her best come-hither look. "Please, Chase…"

She saw his eyes run down the length of her naked body, felt the heat between them. He wanted her. He'd wanted her for longer than any of the others, she was almost sure of that. And yet he still wouldn't have sex with her, not even now.

"Get under the blankets, Lacey," he ordered.

"Why?" She reached down and ran her fingertip down the seam of her pussy lips, seductively parting her wet slit. Her clit was tingling with need. That machine had filled her over and over, but it had left her clit desperate for stimulation. She hadn't been able to touch the hungry little bud until now and as she did a spark of pure pleasure raced through her body. Fuck, yes. She was ready to make love with everything she had.

"Because I said so. Do you want a spanking?"

Lacey scowled at him. "No, I want a fucking."

"You're going to get your butt warmed if you don't start doing as you're told. Get into bed now."

"No." She sat up. "Why don't you want me?"

"I do want you," he sighed. "It's getting late. We can talk about this in the morning."

"I want to talk about it now. Do you think I'm ugly? Or do you think I'm gross because the others have been with me?"

"No. It's not either of those things. I can see you get a lot of pleasure from Rex and Max and Brian. That's a good thing."

"So why not from you?" Her voice cracked. "Chase, you have to tell me something. It feels like you just don't want me, and I can't take that."

He looked at her for a long moment. "I was the one who found you in Venezuela."

"Yeah…"

"I was the one who carried you out of there. I was the one who saw…" He hesitated. "Evidence of what they'd done to you."

Lacey knew she had been a mess when he saved her. She didn't even really remember all of it. Trauma was odd that way. She had no doubt that he probably remembered how it had been when she was found better than she did. But she still didn't understand what that had to do with things now… unless…

"Oh, I get it," she said, suddenly furious. "You don't want to be with me because every time you look at me, you see a victim. You define me by what those assholes did to me."

"No… I…"

"I'm broken to you, aren't I. I'll always be broken to you. Fuck! Chase! I thought you were being sweet to me because you liked me, not because you felt sorry for me."

Lacey couldn't believe this. She had left her past in the past. She'd moved on. It hadn't been easy, and sometimes she had her flashback moments, but she'd worked damn hard not to let those two horrible weeks define the rest of her existence.

"Do you know how hard it is to get over something like that? To just feel normal? It took me so fucking long not to think that I was ruined forever. But I did it. And Rex and Max and Brian, they don't see me as a victim. Hell, I prefer Col thinking I'm an evil bitch to you thinking I'm too pathetic to fuck."

His face twisted in a way that made him look pitying in spite of all the words coming out of his mouth. "I don't think you're pathetic. There's more to this than you can really see right now."

"So tell me."

"I can't."

She got out of bed. "I'm tired of this, Chase. It's been a week and you treat me like I'm made of glass. I'm not. I'm not broken. What they did to me there was awful, but it didn't destroy me. And it won't, unless you keep treating me like it did."

"You're sleeping with three men," he said. "Well, two and a half if you count the machine."

"So?"

"Well…" He paused, not saying the words she knew he wanted to say. Again, she was left to fill in the blanks. Her mind did so at lightning quick speed. He thought the only reason she was alright with any of this was the fact that she'd been hurt by men before. He thought she was a dirty broken slut. He just didn't have the balls to say it.

"Holy shit!" she practically exploded. "You're judging me for that? Seriously. You put me in this situation and now you sit there and act like I'm fucked up because I adapted to it? Fuck you, Chase."

She slammed out of the room and went to the next one down the hall. It happened to be Max's room. He must have left the lounge at the same time they did and was already asleep after his evening of drinking, and didn't really stir as she came in. She got into bed with him and curled up under what she could retrieve of the blankets.

Max snored.

She lay awake all night, listening to the rumble and occasionally grabbing a bit of sheet or blanket when she could in between Max rolling and yanking it off her. She was tempted to go back to Chase's room, but she didn't think she could even look at him now.

She got up early, exhausted from lack of sleep and drank some coffee curled up in the corner of the lounge. The fucking machine was still there. She stared at it, remembering everything Chase had said to her. She'd submitted to Brian's ropes and she'd allowed herself to enjoy that machine. She'd been open and vulnerable in front of them all… and the whole time Chase had been silently sitting there chalking it up against her, taking it as evidence of some deep internal damage.

Well, fuck him. Fuck all of them. She put her cup down, grabbed the dildo off the metal shaft, and threw it as hard as she could. She wasn't aiming at anything in particular, she was just so angry she had to throw something. It hit the floor and bounced up, wriggling in an almost comical way thanks to its schlongy construction. Lacey watched, amused and horrified as it arced through the air and smashed through the window, sending a shower of glass out onto the porch and letting cool morning air rush inside.

The sound of broken glass brought everybody into the room, like a bunch of shatter-activated jack-in-the-boxes.

"What the hell is going on?" Rex demanded. He was shirtless as usual, his torso rippling as he put his hands on his hips and glowered at her.

"The dildo attacked the window," she said as Max, Chase, Col, and Brian stared at her. Chase opened his mouth, but she beat him to the punch.

"I'm not sleeping with any of you ever again. Chase thinks I'm a broken whore."

"What?" Max frowned. "What the?"

Rex sighed and pointed down the hallway. "Go to my room, Lacey. Last one on the right."

She stomped away, leaving the stunned men behind her.

Rex's room was different from the others. It was larger and contained a desk with a laptop on it, as well as a wall full of shelves and books. The bed was covered in handwoven blankets that looked homemade and old.

She stopped just inside the door, impressed.

Rex's palm landed on her still naked backside and urged her further into the room.

"Well, young lady," he said. "I guess I don't need to tell you that breaking windows isn't acceptable behavior."

"It was an accident," she said, backing away from him. "It was a dildo mishap."

He didn't smile.

"I take it you and Chase are having some kind of disagreement," he said. "I'm not going to get involved in that. But I will say this. You don't have to sleep with anyone you don't want to. That includes all of us or any of us."

"You said that was the cost of you looking out for me."

"That's not the case anymore," Rex said. "We've found another way to make it worth our while."

"How?"

"That's not important. What's important is you know you have a choice."

Lacey narrowed her eyes. Rex didn't seem to understand

how well calibrated her bullshit detector was. "I have a choice because you say I do. You said I didn't have a choice and I didn't have a choice, now you say I do and I do. And tomorrow maybe I won't again. That's not choice, Rex. That's bullshit."

"What you don't have a choice in is speaking to me with respect," Rex continued. "And you don't have a choice in destroying property."

He sat down on the edge of the bed and tapped his thigh. "Come here."

Lacey looked at him and shook her head. When she spoke, she sounded less angry and a lot smaller.

"I don't wanna."

"Come here," Rex repeated, his voice softer, but more demanding. She squirmed on the spot, then extended her hand to him and allowed him to draw her closer. She felt herself going over his thighs and just surrendered to the momentum. She was too tired and sad to fight. Chase's reaction had left her devoid of energy and frankly she didn't care what Rex did to her.

"Now listen to me," he said, palming her rear. "I know this isn't easy for you, and I'll give you credit, my girl, you've been a real trouper. I didn't know how you'd fit in, but you've done a damn good job of sticking to your end of the deal. So it's a pity I'm going to have to tan your hide for breaking that window."

With that, he started to spank her. Firm swats landed against her cheeks, stinging her rear, but there wasn't any real force in them, not really. This was a sort of ceremonial spanking, as far as she could tell. He had to do something to her to maintain discipline, but he wasn't tearing her ass up, and for that she was grateful.

"You're going to have to work on keeping your temper," he lectured. "I can't have you breaking windows every damn time someone here upsets you, just like I can't have my boys busting their things up when they get mad. I don't tolerate destructive behavior, you understand, little lady?"

"Yessir," she mumbled, knowing that's what he wanted to hear. There was never any point explaining anything to Rex. He laid down the law and everyone around him obeyed or took the consequences. It was all so easy—except when it wasn't.

"I don't think I've really got your attention, girl," he said, palming her ass again.

"I understand I'm not supposed to break things," she said to the floor. "I know I fucked up."

"Yep," Rex agreed. "You absolutely did. But, in the grand scheme of things, it's a minor mess. Though getting a glazier out here is a real pain in the ass, I hope you realize." He slapped her ass again and she smiled a little.

"I'm sorry," she said, kind of actually meaning it. "I didn't mean to. The dildo ricocheted off the floor."

"That's what rubber projectiles do," Rex said gruffly. "You have to make sure whatever you aim them at has the ability to absorb the force."

With that, he started spanking her again, still not overly hard, but hard enough to sting. "See the way your butt absorbs the force of these slaps," he said. "That's because it's nice and soft. So remember next time you feel the need to throw a sex toy, go for a cushion or a bed."

"Yes, sir, thank you, sir," she giggled, earning herself a harder slap.

"Now don't you start thinking I'm going soft on you," he added. "I'm giving you the benefit of the doubt here. Whatever's going on between you and Chase will have to be resolved."

"I don't think it can be. He thinks I'm a stupid whore for being with you... *ow*!"

He'd spanked her a whole lot harder, leaving a serious sting in the wake of the slap.

"I don't believe for a second that he said that, or that he thinks that. And I won't hear you say that about yourself either."

"Fine," she sighed. "It doesn't matter if Chase doesn't

want me. None of it matters."

"You got a real thing for him, huh?" Rex patted her butt.

"I don't know. Maybe I just don't like being judged."

"He's not judging you," Rex said. "Chase is a gentleman. He was raised right. He's never banged a single whore…"

Lacey winced. That's what she was. A whore. Rex had just said it too.

"Now don't you start thinking that's what we think of you," he growled, catching the thought before it had time to propagate into another fit of temper. "I'm just saying, he doesn't get into sexual relationships quickly, and you've only been with us a week, girl. You can't judge him the way you'd judge Max and me."

"Because you've been bagging whores for years, right?" she replied with an arch laugh.

He slapped her bottom. "Language, young lady."

"That's not fair! That's what you said!"

"Nope, not fair and I don't care," Rex drawled. "I want to see a smile on that face, girl. You have nothing to be sad about. You've got five men looking after you as best we can, and we might not always know how to say everything right, but we're doing our best."

He eased her off his lap and patted the bed. "Climb in and get some sleep," he said. "You're tired, and you're chaotic when you're tired."

He really did know her well. Lacey climbed beneath the covers, grateful for the opportunity to sleep, and for the fact that she could do so without a seriously aching ass.

CHAPTER FIFTEEN

Chase

"Way to ruin a good thing, Chase," Max snorted as he and Chase worked to clean up the glass. Brian was boarding up the window. Meanwhile, Col had decided to go for a run, saying that he wasn't to blame for the hysterical dildo-throwing woman.

"What did you say to her?" Brian asked.

Chase gave a sigh. Relationship issues were so much more complicated when there were four other men directly affected by his actions. "I said that I wanted to look after her and that I wasn't going to rush into sex."

"Why would that make her attack my machine?"

"Because she got it into her head that I was saying she's not good enough to sleep with."

"Why do women always hear the thing you definitely didn't say?" Max shook his head.

"Lacey isn't like that," Brian frowned. "She's usually very good at listening. Maybe she's PMSing."

"And the prize for the thing that will get a dildo thrown at his head if she hears him saying that goes to Brian!" Max chortled. "That's even worse than whatever stupid shit

Chase said to her."

"Why?"

"You can't ever say a woman is PMSing," Max said knowledgeably. "You can't ever mention her period has anything to do with her emotions, even if she's taking a hacksaw to everything. You have to be supportive and stuff and say things like 'that sounds really hard' and 'yes, dear, she probably does deserve to die, more candy?'"

Chase snorted, his mood lifted by Max's inane comments. It was impossible to take anything seriously when Max was offering advice on it.

"I don't know why that is," Brian puzzled as he hammered another nail in. "I mean, if we had significant hormonal fluctuations causing us to retain water and become more sensitive, we'd deal with it, right? We'd have a strategy or something."

"A tactical hot water bottle and a strategic chick-flick collection?" Max laughed.

"That's actually not a bad idea," Brian mused. "I might put something together. If she's going to stay with us, we're going to have to learn her cycles. I'm guessing by her receptivity earlier this week that she was ovulating."

Max winked at Chase and murmured under his breath. "She's going to literally kill him when he pulls this shit on her."

"I don't know," Chase said. "Being prepared is a good idea. We don't really have a whole lot for her."

"What do women need that we don't have? Some of that crunchy dried flowery stuff that tastes bad?"

"Potpourri," Brian said. "My grandmother makes her own."

"I don't think Lacey's really a potpourri sort of girl," Chase said.

"Knitting stuff," Max said, frowning. "And baking… girls like to bake."

"How is it that you both have your ideas of what women like formed by media before you were even born? She's not

June Cleaver. She likes what we like," Chase said.

"Sex, football, and farts. Got it," Max said, giving Chase a thumbs-up.

"Oh, my god, are you still talking about her?" Col was back from his run and was not impressed. He came up the stairs, stretched, and scowled at them all. "All you guys do is talk about her. Lacey. Lacey. Lacey. Lacey's vagina. Lacey's hair. Oh, my god, did you hear what Lacey did?" Col put on a terrible version of a valley girl accent. "You're obsessed."

"Fine," Chase said, doing one last sweep for shards. "What do you want to talk about?"

"Well, I need to get out of here in a couple of days," Col said. "I've got some private stuff I need to take care of. There is life outside Lacey; crazy, I know."

"Talk to Rex about that," Max said. "Daddy will tell you if you're allowed out."

"Don't start calling him that," Col growled. "It's gross enough when she does it."

"I think it's kinda hot," Max grinned.

"We've got the drop tomorrow and then we should be good, right?" Col ignored Max's comment.

"Maybe," Brian said as Chase fell silent. He didn't like this plan at all. "If the CIA can use the information, we may see movement on the people looking for Lacey more or less immediately. If not, it could be a little longer."

"But they can use it, right? This can be over within the week? We can get back to our actual lives?"

"What do you have to do that's so important?"

"None of your fucking business," Col snapped. "I just have a life outside the easy vagina you're all worshipping."

Max and Chase advanced on him as one man, forcing Col off the porch.

"Don't talk about her like that," Max snarled.

"Maybe you should just get out of here now," Chase suggested grimly. "She has enough problems without someone like you judging her."

"Oh, right, because you all respect her soooo much you pass her around like a piñata," Col snapped back.

"Sex is fun, Col, you should try it sometime."

Brian's deadpan comment made Max and Chase burst out laughing while Col glowered at them. The tension was broken for the moment anyway, and fortunately Rex returned before things could escalate any further.

"How is she?" Chase asked him.

"She's fine. Taking a nap. When she wakes up, you should go talk to her."

"She wants to talk to me?"

"I didn't say that. I said you should go and talk to her."

• • • • • • •

Chase waited a few hours and then went to wake Lacey up with a cup of hot chocolate.

"Hey, sleepy," he said as she sat up, her dark hair all askew.

"Hey," she said cautiously, looking at him under her lashes as he put the mug down on the cabinet next to the bed. He sat down on the edge of the bed, his knee drawn up so he could face her as she sat there hiding behind her hair like a wary little animal.

"I do need to talk to you," he said. "I never meant to make you feel broken, Lacey. That's the last thing I wanted to do. You're the strongest woman I've ever known, and I have nothing but admiration for you. I just want to look after you. Is that such a bad thing?"

"Yes," she said, shaking her hair out of her eyes. "When it means that you treat me like I'm totally sexless, it is a bad thing. I fucking… I've wanted you for a long time, Chase. When I was recovering, and feeling bad, when I'd have nightmares… the memory of you coming through that door was all that kept me sane. It reminded me that things could get better. And now it's like… the one man I really want, I can't have, because that did break something. It broke us."

"No, it didn't," he said, reaching out and running his hand through her hair. "Lacey, I love you."

Before she could reply, he pressed a passionate kiss to her lips, tasting her sweetness. He pulled her close as the kiss deepened, her lips parting to allow his tongue entrance as he took her mouth with intense passion. He needed this. She needed this. He could feel his cock stirring in his pants. He'd been in hell for days trying to resist her. Maybe it was time to give in...

"There hasn't been a day since I met you that I haven't thought about you," he breathed roughly, barely containing himself. "I love you, Lacey. I have from the minute I laid eyes on you. And I'm sorry if you don't understand that and you want to twist it into me treating you like a victim just because I don't use your pussy like the others do, but you're just going to have to take my word for it."

"No."

"What?"

Her fingers curled in his shirt. "Show me. Please, Chase. Show me. Just be with me. Please."

Chase pulled off his clothes. She was naked. He would be too. The others usually didn't bother taking anything off to fuck her. They'd just pull their dicks out and go to town, but this wasn't about dominating her or controlling her. This was about giving them both what they'd wanted for too long.

She lay back and spread herself for him, the expression in her milky brown gaze so beautiful he couldn't resist kissing her as he slid between her thighs and let his cock trail down the hot seam of her lips.

"I love you," he murmured against her mouth. God. He had waited so long to say those words and now he couldn't stop saying them.

"I love you too," she whimpered back, rolling her hips beneath him. He held himself on the brink of her pussy, just as he'd held himself on the brink of being with her for so long. This moment mattered. He'd never forget it, and he wanted to be sure she never would too. His kiss was passionate as he drove forward, her wet heat welcoming him as he finally claimed his woman.

He was inside her, joined to her physically the way he'd felt joined with her spiritually since the day he found her. Three years of desire came to culmination as he thrust in and out of her, her sweet body undulating beneath him. This wasn't the rough rutting he'd seen her take from the others. This was passionate lovemaking; this was the kind of sex that transcended every care and concern in the world. As he held her in his arms, looked down into her eyes, and held himself deep inside her, he felt as though he'd loved her forever, for a thousand lifetimes, and he'd love her for a thousand more. She was the only woman in the world to him. She was everything.

"I want you to come inside me, Chase," she said, her voice husky and soft. "I want you to be the first one who counts there."

The thought of coming inside her almost sent him over the edge then and there. Her bare pussy was clenching him, her soft body was wrapped around him, her legs locked around his back. She wanted him. He could see the need in her eyes, feel it in her voice. There was something between them that neither would ever have with another.

"You're sure?"

"Please," she whimpered, arching her back and rolling her hips. Her inner walls gripped him, milked him. He wasn't in control. She was. Her body commanded his, her muscles working his cock until he let out a shout of orgasm and came inside her, his seed flowing deep inside. He could feel her quivering, her clit grinding up against his pubic bone as she worked his seed deeper inside herself, her orgasm sucking it further into her body.

This was reckless. He'd just flooded her bare cunt with billions of virile swimmers. He'd claimed her in a way none of the others had dared, and she'd taken him because he was the mate she truly chose above all others.

He held her close, keeping his cock deep inside her as he softened. "I'll last longer next time," he promised breathlessly.

"After Brian's machine, I can tell you longer isn't always better." Lacey squirmed beneath him. His cum was starting to slip out of her and slide between their glistening bodies. "That was perfect, Chase, thank you."

"Don't thank me," he said, kissing her. "I'm sorry I ever made you feel less than worthy of everything I have."

"You made it up to me," she smiled.

A sharp knock at the door startled both of them. "You better damn well be talking in there!" Rex's rough voice came from the door.

"Shit!" Lacey giggled as Chase rushed his clothes back on.

"We're coming, hold on!" Chase called out. He grabbed her out of bed by the hand and went to open the door. Rex was standing there, his arms over his chest.

"Tell me you didn't just fuck on my bed," he growled.

"Sorry, Daddy, I'll change the sheets," Lacey grinned.

"You bet you will, brat!" Rex reached out and slapped her ass. "Get out of here."

Smiling at how she teased Rex and called him Daddy, Chase led Lacey out of Rex's bedroom and back to his own. He was starting to get a second wind.

CHAPTER SIXTEEN

Lacey

Something was happening.

Rex had ordered her to be tied up and put into the back of the van. He'd walked in that morning and given the order before they were even out of bed. She was still half asleep as Chase got the rope and started to follow directions.

"Why are you doing this?" She squirmed sort of half-heartedly away from him, only to be yanked back toward him. She was wearing one of his t-shirts and underwear, nothing else, which made the prospect of being taken out in public this way all the more galling.

Chase snugged the rope around her ankles. "Daddy's orders," he said with a smile.

"Daddy has some fucked-up orders," Lacey complained, wriggling around to make his job more difficult. She really didn't like being bound. Being unable to run away if she needed to scared the hell out of her. "Why do I have to be tied up? You're going to put me in a cage anyway. There's not even a seatbelt back there. It's unsafe. Just put me in the back seat with you."

"Rex has his orders for a reason," Chase said. "Put your

hands out."

"No," she frowned. "I need my hands."

"Lacey…" He raised a brow at her.

"Seriously, Chase. Don't tie me up. What if something happens? What if there's a car crash and someone hits the back of the van and I get squished like a dead sardine and I can't even run away?"

"Are dead sardines known for their ability to run away?"

"Chase…"

"Okay, hold on."

She sat on the bed and waited as Chase went out to negotiate on her behalf. A second or two later they were both back.

Rex came into the room his hands on his hips, a no-nonsense scowl on his face. "You're going be tied up, because we're going to be undertaking serious work today and I cannot have you jeopardizing it. You can sit in the back seat with Chase, and have a seatbelt, but you're going to be bound, and you're going to be gagged."

"Why?"

"Exactly," Rex said, spinning on his heel. He left the room, and her confused.

"What?"

"He means he doesn't want to be questioned," Chase said, working the rope back around her body. "He takes work very seriously."

"Well, okay, but…"

"Very, very seriously. Lacey, we're mercenaries. We can't have distractions. This really is for everybody's good."

She sat quietly as he worked the rope around her body, securing her ankles together, then running the rope up over her back and then around down between her legs.

"This isn't how you tie people up."

"It is if you want to make it fun for them," Chase said with a little wink. He kept working the rope around her, catching her arms nice and snug next to her body, not forcing them in front or behind. The rope came down around between her legs another two times, wound up around her shoulders, under her breasts, and finally he was done.

She couldn't move, so he picked her up and carried her out over his shoulder, and then she realized the devilish brilliance of his rope work. Every time she moved, the rope ran over her panty-covered pussy. A small movement made the rope move a little; a bigger squirm made it slide more and tighten around her breasts. She was effectively harnessed as well as restrained, her erogenous zones linked with hemp.

The mood among the men was different than she had seen it all week. There was little levity. They were all absolutely focused. She didn't know what the mission was, and she didn't ask. Chase hadn't gagged her and she didn't want anyone to notice that fact.

They were wearing relatively casual clothes, but they were also packing heat. So nothing super militaristic, but obviously still something dangerous. Lacey keep her eyes on them as Chase loaded her into the back seat of the van and strapped her in with a seatbelt.

A few minutes later they set off, left the forest, and headed out into the countryside. The mood was solemn and for the most part they were silent. There was no chatter at all, which she found kind of strange. Usually you couldn't shut Max up, and Col was almost always making some dark crack at her or someone else. But there was nothing.

Lacey was excited to see what was going to happen. She was also excited because every jolt of the van made the rope move between her legs and stimulated her pussy. If Chase had intended it to be a distraction for her, it worked. Her hips squirmed slowly in the seat all the way to their destination, which turned out to be an old dumping ground for wrecked cars—it was about as ominous a place as she could imagine.

Someone was waiting for them.

Two black SUVs were parked next to a burned-out

Mustang, and six or so men were standing around in dark suits and dark sunglasses even though the day was overcast.

Lacey kept her mouth firmly shut as Max brought the van to a halt a few dozen feet away. This was exciting as hell. They were meeting with government officials. CIA, if she had to guess. They had a more furtive air about them than the FBI. The FBI liked to strut about in their heavily marked windbreakers at every available opportunity. The CIA, on the other hand, weren't supposed to be operating within US borders.

Rex and Brian got out of the van and proceeded toward the men. Max, Col, and Chase hung back a bit, but were also out and ready. Lacey suddenly saw precisely how the unit worked. Rex led. Brian provided tactical. The other three were muscle and danger. And they looked it. She squirmed more, her pussy grinding against the rope as she looked on breathlessly.

Were Rex and crew getting information about a job? Surely not. There was no reason to meet to get a job. Unless lines couldn't be secured. Maybe there was something that had to be passed on in person. It was hard to make out what they were saying. From a distance she had some chance of reading lips, but the tinted windows added an extra challenge, and she could only see one of the men's mouths. Concentrating really hard, Lacey tried to make out what he was saying. *Red tough dingoes swim curtains*? No. That couldn't be it.

A second later, she saw Brian hand something over. Okay. Not a job. It was a drop-off. A drop-off of what, though? For the last week, they hadn't done anything but look after her. Had they been holding on to something that whole time? It was possible. The world didn't revolve around her, after all.

In spite of her rational thoughts, a horrible sensation of nausea began to rise through her. She'd given Brian access to her materials. He'd claimed to have deleted them, but what if... no. She pushed the thought away. They wouldn't do that to her. That would be incredibly shitty.

She sat up as the spooks and Rex came walking over to the back of the van. Did she have something to do with this after all? Rex opened the van door and several spooks looked in at her as if she was some kind of interesting exhibit.

"This is her," he said. "You can ask her anything you need to with regard to the data."

"Like hell you can!" Lacey practically exploded with indignation as the full realization of what was happening blew up inside her. She had been right. They had taken her data. They hadn't destroyed it and ended the feud with Senator Fishland. They'd fucking traded it. "You double-crossed me, you asshole!"

"She's a little mouthy," Rex said. "But she settles down if you treat her right. We can lend her to you for a couple of days if you need."

The lead agent nodded impassively "We'll be in touch if we need her to corroborate anything."

Rex shut the door, leaving her fuming. Now she knew why they'd tied her up, even though she hated it. They didn't want her loose when she realized how bad she'd been screwed over.

Fuck this. Fuck them. Every single one of them. Lacey could not believe this shit.

She started to swear, loud and aggressively, and to kick at the sides of the van as hard as she could. The action made the rope scrape across her pussy too hard to be pleasurable, but she didn't care, she was angry as hell and they were going to pay. Oh, fucking hell yes, were they going to pay.

"Settle down!" Chase jumped into the van next to her and stilled her legs.

"Absolutely not," she hissed.

"You'll be gagged again."

"Like I give a fuck."

Chase sighed and closed the van door behind him so he was trapped in there with Lacey and her rage. The others were still outside, conferring like the traitors they were.

"I'm sorry," he said grimly. He didn't look happy about the situation, but she didn't care what he was feeling.

"How could you do this to me? I trusted you."

"I know," he said, the corners of his mouth downturned. "But this is for the best, Lacey. For all of us."

"How? How is this the best? How is taking everything I intended to go to the public and handing it to the people who bury this shit in the shadows best for anyone?"

"It will hopefully get the others off your back. No more assassination attempts in shitty motels. You might be able to get your life back."

"Or I might not, because they might sit on that information for years. That's the fucking CIA. They don't care whether I live or die. They'll use that information for their own ends. Senator Fishland will probably get blackmailed by them now, so he'll only come after me harder." Her eyes were foggy with tears of betrayal and frustration. "How could you, Chase?"

"There's five of us in this unit, but Rex makes the ultimate decisions."

"So you're just his bitch, is that it? Rex sells me out and you don't even warn me? You just let it happen?"

"First, Rex didn't sell you out. He passed your data on to the people best placed to do something about it. Second, call me that again and you will be a very sore little girl."

He looked serious, his blue eyes a darker hue than usual. Chase had never spanked her. Chase had never touched her except in a tender way. She almost didn't believe he had it in him.

"Whatever," she said, turning her head away. "You could have warned me."

"And what would that have done? You would have argued, you would have gotten into trouble, probably ended up beaten with someone's belt, or maybe more, and the outcome would have been the same. Rex knows what he's doing. We trust him because he doesn't lead us wrong. And he won't lead you wrong either."

She gritted her teeth. Lacey didn't have a slavish devotion to Rex. He was hot, but that wasn't enough to make her give her natural independence up and just hand every decision over to him. He'd lied to her. They'd all outright lied to her. That wasn't forgivable.

Staying utterly silent, she said nothing at all as Rex and the others got into the van. The ride back to the cabin was undertaken in a heavier silence than the ride out to the wrecker's yard. Maybe they felt guilty for fucking her over. Maybe they didn't. Maybe they could go fuck themselves.

"Untie me, please," she asked Chase grimly when they arrived back at the cabin.

Chase took a knife and cut the ropes off her. They fell to the floor of the van, loose and limp and pathetic, just like the feelings she'd had for these men. She'd slept with them. She'd given herself to them. She'd trusted them. And each and every one of them had lied to her face and stolen from her.

Maybe she deserved it after going back on her word in Venezuela. Maybe this was their idea of poetic justice. She didn't know and she didn't care.

She got out of the van without another word, keeping her eyes to herself. She couldn't so much as look at these men now, but she heard them mumbling to one another when they thought she was out of earshot.

"She already knows? How?" Rex was asking the most stupid question in the world. For a second she was stunned at how dim he was being, then she realized it wasn't that *he* was stupid. It was that he didn't give *her* credit for having two brain cells to rub together.

"She worked it out. She's a journalist," Chase said. "You took a journalist to a drop. Should have left her back at the house with me and one of the others like I suggested."

So he had been in on it too all along. Dear, sweet, lying asshole Chase.

"We needed all of you," Rex growled. "You couldn't

have just blindfolded her?"

"She panics badly enough when we tie her up without blindfolding her too," Chase said. "Besides, you brought them right up to the van and told them they could have her. That wasn't part of the deal."

Lacey kept walking. She didn't want to hear the rest of the conversation. She didn't want to hear a damn thing out of a single damn one of their damn mouths ever again. She wanted to be by herself. She wanted to think. There was only one spare room in the house—the room that wasn't a room.

She went to the closet and put herself away in the holding cell, shutting the door behind her.

"So she's pissed," Max noted from outside the door.

Their voices still carried, unfortunately. She lay down on the uncomfortable cot bed and stared into the darkness, tears forming in her eyes. Betrayal sat like a weight in her stomach. She could never trust them again after this. Everything that had been building up between them was over.

This was the end of everything as far as she was concerned. Their protection was meaningless, just a front to extract data from her and funnel it to the CIA. She wouldn't be surprised if they cut her loose in a day or two when they were sure they'd gotten everything they needed from her.

"You blame her?" Chase replied. "She feels betrayed and lied to."

"She'll get over it." Rex's rumble galled her the most.

Wrong.

She would not get over this. In fact, she now had every intention of doing what she should have done in the beginning, before she got scared and called these men for help.

• • • • • •

Her quiet, searing anger seemed to keep the men at bay

throughout the rest of the day and into the evening. She was hungry and thirsty, but she didn't emerge from the cell until very early the next morning. Hours of darkness had focused her anger and helped her formulate a plan.

It was about four in the morning when Lacey got up out of her cage, found her leggings and her shoes, got dressed, and fixed herself breakfast. She went and sat on the porch by herself, eating and drinking before the rest of them got up—most of them anyway. About ten minutes after she sat down, Col emerged from the forest at a jog. He was shirtless, his torso rippling in the early morning light.

He stopped in front of the porch and stretched against a tree, his body moving in a perfect symphony of muscular hotness. They didn't say anything to one another. Lacey put her head down and chewed her cereal while he stretched as if he was all alone, then walked up past her and went into the cabin.

It was the final straw.

She was less than nothing to that man, but maybe he was the most honest of them all. Col didn't pretend to be one thing and then betray her by being another. He had never, for a second, made her think that he liked her. Not like Rex, and Chase, and Max, and Brian. Brian was the worst offender. He'd lied right to her face without any kind of compunction at all. Chase was the only one who seemed to feel a bit guilty about it, but guilt was too little, too late.

Lacey got up and walked to the van. She knew that it was a waste of time. It wasn't as if they'd just leave the keys in the... ignition.

They were there. Hanging down next to the steering wheel. It was as if the universe itself was saying, *hey, ditch these assholes, let's go for a ride.*

Lacey got into the van, turned the key, and started it. To her shock, the engine actually kicked into life. The next few seconds seemed to play out like hours as everything happened all at once.

A moment after the engine started, Col came bursting

out of the cabin. She already had the van in reverse. He ran up at an impressive sprint and wrenched at the door. He even managed to get it open before she could lock it, but he was too late. She slammed the van into first gear and put her foot down. The engine screamed to the red line almost instantly, forcing another hard shift as it rocketed away, leaving Col tumbling behind her in the dirt.

For a brief moment she was afraid that she'd hit him, but she saw in the rearview mirror that he'd rolled up to his feet and looked to be unharmed. Good. She didn't need another death on her conscience.

CHAPTER SEVENTEEN

Rex

"Who left the keys in the van?" Rex demanded. A full scale mission of closing the stable door after the horse had bolted was underway as they stood around with their dicks in their hands, doing sweet fuck all. Lacey had taken their only means of transportation. Usually they'd have more cars available but this whole mission had been undertaken on the fly, and having their van stolen wasn't on the agenda.

"That would be Max," Col said. "He was driving it last."

"Where is Max?"

"He's trying to start the ATV we have in the shed."

"I don't think we're going to run her down on that," Rex sighed. What a shit show. They were now in the very unenviable position of having to wait for someone to bring them another car, an associate who did some delivery work for them sometimes.

"At least we can trace the van, which means we can trace her," Brian said. While the rest of them had run around looking for ways to chase her in vain, Brian had done what he always did, gone for his laptop and opened the tracking program on the van. "She's headed into the city, I think."

"Why would she go back there?"

"She's a city girl," Chase said. "And she's smart enough to know that high pop areas are good places to hide."

"Not when you're wanted by a cabal," Col replied. "I think she's just pissed off and looking to make a statement. That's what she always does."

"Oh, because you know her so well," Chase replied. "You were the last one to see her, weren't you, Col. You didn't know she was about to bolt?"

"I didn't know the van had the fucking keys in it," Col shot back. "I always said she should be locked up, not left to wander around."

"She's not our prisoner," Chase said. "She hasn't done anything wrong. There was no reason to treat her like a captive. And there wouldn't have been a problem if we hadn't damn well lied to her about what we were going to do with the information she had."

"That wasn't her decision to make," Rex said. "She put her life and her data in our hands. We make the decisions, not her. And when we get her back, we're going to damn well teach her that."

It had been a very long time since anyone had defied Rex on this level. He wasn't actually sure he'd ever experienced insubordination like this. Lacey might not have liked his decision to keep her information and pass it on, but that was tough shit as far as he was concerned.

Years of military experience had given him a serious blind spot. Civilians didn't have obedience built into them. He hadn't seen Lacey's rebellion coming because he'd mistaken her sexual submission for real discipline—and the fact that she hadn't thrown a tantrum yesterday had only lulled him further into the false belief that she would do as he said even if she didn't like it.

He was disappointed, in himself and in Lacey. They were going to get her back, and when they did, he was going to teach her one hell of a lesson she'd never forget. Obedience, discipline, submission. He'd instill every single one of them into her at the end of his belt, and whatever else came to hand. Hell, she'd ask him for permission to fart by the time he was done with that little brat.

CHAPTER EIGHTEEN

Col

Tension was in the air and Col didn't care for it. This whole thing with Lacey Christie had been a mistake from the beginning. They should never have offered to help her, and they definitely never should have gotten mixed up in the senatorial shit show that she was involved with.

When he'd seen her that morning, he'd been tempted to say something, but what was there to say? *Sorry we fucked you over, sucks, right?* That wouldn't have helped. And it probably wouldn't have changed the outcome any either.

They managed to get a new van out about an hour later. As soon as the contractor drove it up, they all piled into it and headed to Washington. Most of the journey was undertaken in silence. Max was quiet because he knew he'd fucked up, Brian was never a loud guy, Rex was seething, and Chase was so worried about Lacey that he looked sick.

"Alright," Rex said when they dropped their contractor off. "We're going to head after the van…"

"It stopped moving half an hour ago," Brian said. "I think she's out of it."

"Well, we'll start at the van."

"She'll be at a TV studio, or a radio station," Col said.

Nobody listened to him. They were all talking over one another. Max thought she'd have gone back to her apartment. Chase thought she was headed to a CIA office. Rex just wanted the van back as far as Col could tell.

"Brian and I will go get the van," Rex said. "You three drive around to her apartment."

When Rex and Brian had headed off in an Uber, Col got out of the van.

"What are you doing?" Chase asked him, frowning.

"I've got an idea where she is," Col said. "I'll call you if it pans out."

"But Rex said…"

Col shut the van door and headed off in his own direction. Sometimes he really hated the team aspect of their job. It was great when Rex was right, but when Rex was wrong it could lead to hours, days, or even weeks of chasing their own asses. He knew where Lacey was. There was only one place pissed-off journalists ever went: public.

He followed his intuition all the way to Washington DC's most prominent news studio. It wasn't easy to gain access without being detected. There were cameras everywhere of all kinds, but he made it through to the news room and there he found Lacey. She'd been given a white blouse and a cute pink pencil skirt and she'd been put through hair and makeup. She looked gorgeous. And she was about to make the biggest, most unredeemable mistake of her life if he didn't intervene in…

Four… three… two… The producer started counting down.

Col pulled his balaclava down and went in.

• • • • • • •

Earlier today, journalist Lacey Christie was abducted from inside the studio. Watch the shocking moment a man entered the studio and carried her away.

The image on the television in the cabin showed Lacey perched on a stool wearing a pretty silk blouse. She was still wearing it now, though it didn't look as good on a couch in a cabin as it did under studio lights. The interview hadn't actually begun, but a camera was running and it captured the moment when Col came running in, scooped her up over his shoulder, and headed off screen. It all happened in a matter of seconds, so quickly that the syndicating station had slowed it down in order to draw the moment out for the viewers at home.

Col smirked to himself. It had been a clean snatch. He was happy with it. His face was covered and away from the camera at all times so his identity was safe. There was a pretty sweet shot of Lacey's ass caught just as it went past the camera too. Nice.

"Great," Rex thundered. "One of you goes to the *media*. And the other goes blundering into a place with cameras *everywhere* and plays fucking *Rambo*!"

Lacey and Col were sitting side by side on the couch while Rex stalked back and forth in front of them, his hands behind his back, his body occasionally blocking the view as he growled like an animal with every word the announcer said.

"Are you trying to get yourselves killed? Is that it? Have you two decided to join forces to make the worst possible decisions possible?"

Col knew better than to answer him, but Lacey was mouthy.

"I didn't do anything stupid," she said. "I did what I had to do. I made the choice you left me to make."

"So we pass your information on, and you try to go and burn it on television. Do you know what would have happened if you had done that? We were paid for that information on the basis nobody else has it. If you'd have spilled your guts nationwide, we'd owe the agency more than any of us are worth."

"Exactly. I had to get her out of there before she talked,"

Col explained, as footage of him carrying Lacey out of the studio played for about the hundredth time in five minutes. "I didn't have a choice except to go in there and take her. She forced my hand."

"Oh, she forced you to create this scene?" Rex jabbed the remote at the TV.

Police are searching for the independent journalist, who broke the Venezuela conspiracy just three years ago. There are serious concerns for her safety.

The television blared until Rex hit the mute button to shut it up.

"I'm not sorry," Lacey insisted, taking the heat off Col by opening her mouth again. "You lied to me. You told me you'd deleted everything. But you sold it and now you're worried you might not get to keep your blood money."

"We passed it on to the parties who should have had it in the first place," Rex growled. "There are checks and balances for corrupt and criminal senators. There's real recourse. But you wanted your moment in the spotlight, so instead of funneling it to the right channels in the first place, you sat on it and turned yourself into a sitting duck."

"You could have just said that in the first place," Lacey whined. "You didn't have to lie to me!"

Rex shot a vicious glance at her. "Lying to you is easier, because we know what you do with the truth."

"What?"

"You sell it for your own personal glory."

"Fuck you," Lacey snarled, her face contorted. "You have your job, I have mine. I fucking do it. People deserve to know what's going on. They deserve to know who is doing what to who. They deserve…"

"Enough!" Rex thundered. "Don't worry about what the rest of the world deserves. Worry about what you deserve for this stupid stunt. If not for Col, you'd be dead right now."

"Oh, bullshit."

Chase walked up and slapped a picture down the coffee

table in front of them. Col didn't need to look at it. He knew what it was of. Chase explained for Lacey's benefit though. "This is a sniper, located outside the studio on the building across the street. They were everywhere. Col had to go past a team on standby just to get to you. He's just lucky they mistook him for one of theirs."

"What, they have snipers sitting outside every studio now?"

"Senator Fishland's office has phone taps on every media outlet in the city. When you call, they know. It doesn't take much to mobilize men to the right spots. You were seconds away from a head shot. Frankly, I don't know how you managed to get in there without your brains being painted across the wall," Rex growled. "You should be dead a dozen times over, Lacey."

She finally fell silent, petulant.

"As for you, Col." Rex turned his attention back to Col. "I don't like how you did what you did, I don't like this fallout, but I give you credit. If you hadn't done it, we'd be watching execution style footage right now."

"Yeah," Col agreed. "They'd have blown her brains out on live television just to prove a point. I think they were waiting for the feed to go nationwide."

"That would hardly make Fishland look innocent," Lacey grumbled.

"It wouldn't have to make him look innocent. It would send a message to anyone thinking about speaking up that they'd end up dead. This isn't about you, Lacey. It's not even about this senator, or this story. It's about what happens to little girls who don't know when to shut the hell up," Col growled.

Lacey shrank down next to him, scowling to herself. She didn't get it. No matter how much danger she put herself in, she never seemed to get the potential outcome of it. It was like there was a part of her damn brain missing where consequences should be.

"So what now?" she muttered. "Everyone is looking for

me."

"We are going to keep our heads down. We are going to lay low, and we are going to wait until the official channels deal with this properly."

"So that's your big plan?" Her eyes went wide as she started up again with the drama. "Hand all our evidence over and just wait? How do you know the people you gave it to aren't part of this? You don't know how deep the rot goes."

"I know we have money in our accounts. And I know you are not going to go out of our sight for the rest of your damn life!" Rex growled furiously. "You're going to pay for this, Lacey. Every single one of us is going to punish you for this until you learn that there's more than your life on the line. Your principles don't mean shit when they get other people dead."

"I'm sorry!"

"You're not," Rex growled. "But you will be. Col, you start."

CHAPTER NINETEEN

Lacey

Fear zipped through her belly. She'd known she was in serious trouble long before getting back to the cabin and seeing the satellite news feed. The moment Col grabbed her off that stool, she knew she was fucked. She'd been relieved when he duct-taped her hands and feet together, gagged her, and put her in the back of the van in the cage she usually so loathed. At least then she didn't have to talk or explain herself to the five very angry mercenaries who had come for her.

They didn't care why she'd done what she'd done. They cared that she'd put herself in danger. They didn't understand about the ethics of journalism, or the importance of a story being told. They cared about money. Getting it, keeping it, and—she had to admit—using it to keep her safe.

Now there would be no arguing her way out of punishments. There wasn't a single sympathetic face in the room. Least of all Col. Rex had just thrown her to the wolf.

She risked a glance sideways and saw his dark glower. It made her want to curl up on herself and whimper for mercy.

Col was dangerously hot but he also had the least affection for her and the most anger. She was scared of what he would do in the name of punishment.

Col stood up and crooked a finger at her. "Come outside."

She followed him meekly, knowing she didn't really have a choice.

It was cold outside. The chill in the air made her nipples hard and would have caused her to shiver if it weren't for the fear having that effect already. The rest of them stayed indoors. They were leaving her alone with Col. Even Chase wasn't coming out to defend her. She had to face Col's wrath alone.

As she stood and looked at him, she knew this had been a very long time coming. This wasn't just about the events of the last day. This was three years of rage about to be unleashed on her. She didn't know what he had in mind, but she knew it wasn't going to be good.

"You're smart, but you don't know fucking anything," Col began harshly. "I would have thought after getting worked over in Venezuela, you'd be more careful, but you're not. You're careless and you're reckless and it's like you want to die."

"I wasn't in that much danger! I can defend myself."

"You can't defend yourself against a fart," he sneered, his lip curling as he folded his strong arms over his chest. "You're a weak little girl who has to depend on men to defend her, but you don't like the reality of that, so you run around like an idiot screaming how liberated and equal you are. Well, you know what, girl? You're not equal. Not to me. Not to any of us. There's only one way a woman matches a man in combat, and that's if she has a gun. I'll be damned if I trust you with one of those."

"Why? You think I'd use it on you?"

"Wouldn't put it past you," he growled. "You like to turn on people who help you."

Now he was just plain pissing her off. "Fuck you, Col. I

could kick your ass if I wanted to," she snarled.

Col rolled his eyes. "Delusional."

"I could! I've been doing self-defense!"

"Oh, self-defense. Well then, I didn't know you'd learned self-defense," Col guffawed. "I'm sure that totally changes the laws of physics and makes a tiny woman somehow able to fight a man. Come on then, show me how you're going kick my ass before I tear yours up."

After Venezuela, Lacey really had put some serious time into martial arts. Enough time to know that Col was basically right: a woman of her size was not going to fare well against a man like him in a straight-up knock-down fight, no matter how good she was. There were only two ways to succeed: run or fight dirty.

The first one wasn't really an option, seeing as she'd just told him she could defend herself, so she went with the second. It gave her no small measure of pleasure to feint toward his balls, then draw back and slam her fist as hard as she could at his jaw.

The blow never made contact. He turned to the side to parry her feint then grabbed her wrist as it shot forward. The second she felt him capture her arm, she panicked. She tried to pull herself free, but his hand was like iron around her smaller arm. Lacey lashed out with her other fist, but he caught that one too, staring down at her with a dark frown.

It was over in a matter of seconds. Her best shot had been absolutely nothing to him. It had been a lame attempt and she wished she hadn't made it.

"Now what?" Col asked.

"Fuck you," she swore, embarrassed. Truth was, all the self-defense classes in the world weren't going to make her a match for Col. He was built for combat, and she wasn't. She could still kick him in the balls if she wanted to, but they both knew that wouldn't end well.

"You're a hundred and twenty pounds soaking wet," he growled down at her. "I'm two forty. Do you know what I could do to you?"

"Yes!" she screamed. "Yes, I fucking know!"

He jerked her forward against his hard body and snarled down at her. "Do you know what I'm *going* to do to you?"

"Hurt me."

"Yes."

Nose to nose, eye to eye, heat sparked between them, a raw mutual hate that transformed into a brutal kiss. Col grabbed her ass and pulled her hard against him, his other hand in her hair as his tongue lashed inside her mouth, demanding everything she had to give and more. This was not a lover's kiss. This was the kiss of a man who was going to ravage her. Lacey's heart hammered in her chest as Col ripped her clothes off her, tearing the only attire she had into shreds.

His hand squeezed her breast and pushed her back up against a tree. She let out a squeal as his teeth found the nipple and clamped down, holding that sensitive bud in place as his tongue punished it with lashing strokes that made her cry out in pleasure pain.

"They've all had you," Col growled. "But not one of them has fucked you like you deserve to be fucked."

He pulled her legs wide, holding her up off the ground. He yanked her panties to the side, baring her pussy so the hard scimitar of his cock could find her slit. He pushed back and forth, the head of his cock crudely sliding along her slit, gathering her juices.

"You're a little slut," he said as the hot head of his cock found her cold little clit hiding between her outer lips.

When she'd thought Chase thought she was a slut, it had been devastating, but hearing the word out of Col's mouth in those heated, hateful tones made her body run hot with erotic fire. She was a slut. She didn't care. As much as he hated her, he needed her pussy just like the rest of them. He wasn't immune.

"You're wet," he growled, propping her up with one hand and slapping the head of his cock against her pussy with the other. "Why are you so fucking wet?"

"Because I'm a slut," she said, owning the word. "You might be two forty, but I don't need to be. You want me. You're so fucking angry because you don't want to want me."

"Shut up," he growled, covering her mouth with another rough kiss.

She felt his palm slide between her legs, his foot kicking them wider. He gathered her wrists in one hand and pinned her up against the tree, his fingers running along her spread slit. He spanked her pussy over and over again, making her arch and cry out in pain. It hurt. Her sensitive lower lips were swelling under his punishment, but he didn't care. He wanted this to hurt, and maybe she needed it to hurt as well.

"I'm going to fuck you," he growled against her mouth. "I'm going to tear your pussy up, girl."

He thrust roughly up inside her and she screamed out as his cock drove into her, her hair swishing wildly back and forth as he pounded her with remorseless, relentless strokes from the get go.

"Asshole," she hissed as her pussy clamped down around his cock.

"Little bitch," he growled back, kissing her furiously.

She gave him as good as he got, her darkest, wildest animal impulses free as they fucked viciously, her nails raking down his back, her legs wrapped around his hips. She wanted him as much as she hated him. She needed him. She needed this. None of the others would give her this release. Only Col could, because Col didn't care about anything other than ravaging her utterly and completely. He tore into her pussy as his eyes raked into her soul, his cock thrusting so deep she felt him hit her cervix stroke after stroke, punishing her to the core. This was the absolution she had been waiting for, the punishment only he could give.

They were connected. Fully. He was the dark. She was the light. He wanted to overcome her and she wanted him to draw her down into the night she deserved.

"Faithless little slut," he growled. "Lying little bitch."

Every word was accompanied with a devastating thrust that made her pussy ache. Her clit was grinding against his hard pubic bone and she was trapped between his demanding body and the tree behind her, rough bark scratching her back as the mercenary took his pleasure in her soft body, his mouth finding her breasts and her nipples, licking, biting, making her scream out.

"Sadistic fucking asshole!" She threw words back at him even as her pussy clenched and spasmed around his cock, milking him with desperate contractions that demanded he give her everything he had.

Col could not resist. He kissed her roughly, his body slamming into hers as he came inside her, his seed flooding her pussy in thick loads as she wrapped her legs around him, holding him deep inside her.

And then the orgasm faded and they were left standing there, devoid of arousal. He slid from her pussy and let her stand, her aching sex throbbing between her thighs. She could still feel him inside her. She probably would for a long time. He had been rough and merciless, and she had deserved every bit of it.

"Lacey…"

"Yes?"

"I don't hate you," Col said, running his fingers through her hair.

"I know."

He gave her a quizzical look and drew her close, letting her rest her tired body against his. "You do, huh? Cocky little thing."

"You knew where to find me. You've been keeping a closer eye on me than anyone else all this time. You knew where I was going and why, when everyone else thought I was just running away like a crazy woman. You caught me because you get me."

"The best predators know their prey," Col said with a dark smirk. "You bet your ass I knew what you were up to. Someone had to keep an eye on you all this time. The rest of them were so damn distracted by your body. You could have killed them in their sleep if you wanted."

"I'm not a murderer."

"No. You're a tattle-tale. You can't help but run and tell," he said, rubbing her ass. "And I know you're going to try to tell this story one day too, aren't you? You've probably already started writing it in your head."

"I don't have to tell everything," she said. "I've learned my lesson."

"We'll see."

She felt her stomach clench. She wanted him to believe her. Suddenly, it mattered a lot what he thought.

"Col, really, I won't tell. I know you were so angry with me, but so were the others. It was different for you though, and I don't know why, but I know it was, and I'm sorry."

He gave her a long, considering look. "Do you really want to know why I couldn't forgive you like the others did?"

"Yes, please." Her eyes were misty with tears. "Whatever it is, I'm so sorry."

He pulled out his wallet, and then plucked a picture from it and held it out to Lacey. She saw Col, and another younger man who looked a lot like him, but was in a wheelchair.

"This is my brother. He's special needs. I pay for his facility. When we were discharged, I couldn't keep up the payments. He had to move out of the home he liked and into one where they were less careful about his meds and his supervision. Long story short, he overdosed on his medication because he forgot he'd already taken it twice that day. He almost died."

Lacey's stomach clenched with guilt.

"Col... I am so sorry. If I could take it back, I would. I really would. Is he okay now?"

"I got him back into his previous home once we got our first paycheck. He's doing okay."

"The others... Rex and..."

"They don't know."

"They don't know about your brother?"

"Nope," Col said. "I don't talk about family."

"Then I won't say a word about your brother," she promised earnestly. "Not ever. I know you don't think I can keep a secret, but I'll keep this one."

Col gave a little shrug. "It doesn't matter," he said. "I just figured you deserved to know why you had to suffer."

A dark little tingle ran through her body. Yes. He'd made her suffer, and she'd loved every minute of it. Suffering for Col was beautiful and intense. It ached, but it filled a part of her she hadn't known was empty.

Pressing herself to his chest, she looked up into his eyes. "Will I have to suffer again?"

He looked down at her with a dark gaze, his hand cupping her ass roughly. "Oh, god, yes," he promised. "I'm going to take this ass."

"Wha…"

"I want to fuck your asshole," Col repeated. "Hard."

"Oh. Uhm."

"Yeah, not so easy when it's not your pussy in play, is it," Col snorted. "I want to take a part of you that you won't enjoy. I want to whip your ass red and then fuck it until you cry."

He was saying terrible things to her. Terrible, mean things. He wanted to hurt her. He wanted her to cry. He wanted to push his cock inside her dirtiest hole and punish her there too. She was frightened, but she couldn't help pressing against him, smearing his leg with her naughty clit and the mixture of her juices and his cum.

"I just got started with you, girl," Col promised darkly, patting her ass. "Get down on your hands and knees."

She sank down next to him, going to her hands and knees in the dirt. This was filthy and depraved. This was wrong. Col kneeled behind her and she felt him pulling up what remained of the skirt she'd gotten from wardrobe.

"You're covered in cum and dirt," he said, slapping her bare ass hard enough to make her squeal. "You're a filthy little slut, aren't you."

"Yes," she moaned softly.

He pushed the skirt up and she felt him wrap his fist around the gusset of her panties and pull. There was a tearing sound as he ruined her only pair of underwear, and then there was nothing but cool air between him and her.

She felt him scooping up his cum and her juices, pushing it against the tight little bud of her asshole. A whimper escaped her lips as he started pushing his finger there, but he didn't care. He liked it. He wanted it to hurt. He wanted to punish her, and that knowledge only made her pussy wetter.

"You're a bad girl," he growled. "The others don't know how bad. Rex thinks you're a brat. Chase thinks you're an angel. But I know what you are, Lacey. You're a scrappy little liar, you survive because you'll do whatever it takes. You're not weak. You're not broken. You don't need our protection. You'd survive anything and anyone. That's why you keep finding trouble. Because it's in your fucking soul."

He pulled his finger out of her ass and spanked her hard several times, his palm exploding against her bottom with rough slaps that made her scream.

"I will be waiting, Lacey. Every time you fuck up. Every time you disobey. I'm going to have them send you to me, because I'm the only one who can really punish you, aren't I?"

"Yes!" She screamed the word.

"What they do is too gentle, isn't it," he continued, belting her ass with his hand hard enough to make her cry out each and every time. "They tease you and get you close, but they never really satisfy the dark little slut in your soul."

He used his finger on her ass, sawing it in and out as he spanked her harder than she'd ever been spanked in her life. It hurt, but more than that, it transcended pain. It made her warm all over. She was in the dirt, but she was floating too, lighter than she'd ever been before.

When he pulled his finger out and put his cock to her

hole, she let out a feral moan of need. She needed him to fuck her there. She needed to feel him hard and rough inside her ass. She craved it, and he gave it to her, pushing forward steadily.

"Oww, Col… Owwwww, fuck…"

"I know it hurts," he growled softly. "It's supposed to. Let it hurt, Lacey. Don't fight it."

She felt the thick head of him spreading her wider and wider, making her sphincter give way. Suddenly there was a pop of sensation as he pushed past and then his hard shaft was inside her and he was fucking her there, in the place where good girls never got fucked.

He grabbed her hips and used her ass like he'd used her pussy, long strokes that became more intense as her muscle gave way to him and allowed him in, her whimpers and moans only serving to make him harder. He scooped some more wetness out of her pussy, using her cunt like a lube dispenser, and smeared it on his cock as he rode deeper inside her ass.

Lacey was dizzy with desire, her whole body and being caught up in the moment of being fucked and ravaged by this vengeful man who alone knew how to punish her completely. Her hands dug into the dirt as he fucked her harder and rougher, making her scream into the forest with every thrust.

"I'm going to come inside this hole too," he promised. "You're going to drip for me, girl. You're going to ache for me for a long time too. Every time Chase or Max or Rex or Brian sink their dicks inside you, it's me you're going to feel."

She was going to come. She couldn't believe it, but she was on the verge of orgasm. His words were fierce and cruel, his cock was rough inside her ass, but her pussy was aching with desire and her clit was one painful bud of tingling nerves desperate for release as Col pounded her ass to his own roaring orgasm, his dominance over her complete as he shot a fresh load of cum deep into her sore hole.

Lacey screamed as she felt him come. He reached under her and pinched her clit and it was like a button activating a rocket. She screamed with ecstasy and writhed beneath him, her orgasm so powerful she lost consciousness in the midst of it, pleasure and pain and dirt all mixed together in the gathering dark.

She was only half-sensate when she felt him pick her up and hold her in his arms. "Time to get you cleaned up, girl," he murmured. "You've got four other men to fuck."

CHAPTER TWENTY

Max
A day later…

"He's ruined her pussy for the rest of us," Max complained as he gently ran his fingers over Lacey's very well spanked and fucked lower lips. He was sitting in the living room on the couch and she was curled up in his arms naked. She hadn't been allowed clothing since coming back from the city and he quite liked that. What he didn't like as much was how sore she was. She squirmed and made a little whimpering sound as he stroked her in that sensitive little spot. Col had really gone to town on her.

Max expected her to hate Col after all that, but she cuddled up with him as much as she did the rest of them, though she did seem more shy. Couldn't even meet his eye most of the time. Col glanced over at the pair of them and smirked, pleased with himself.

"I thought we all got a turn," Max complained.

"We do," Rex said. "Just not necessarily all at once."

Lacey let out a little moan. She was really going to get it, and for a long time. Nobody was happy with the shit she'd pulled. She was still all over the news too, which pissed Rex off every time he saw it. Max got quite a laugh out of seeing the boss snap the TV off whenever the news came on.

"Max," she whimpered. "You're not mad at me, are you?"

"I'm not mad at you at all. Stealing a van is kind of badass, but you stole my van and the rest of the guys ragged on me for leaving the keys in it, which was a pain in my ass. It fits that I get to be a pain in yours too, huh?"

"But I'm sore," she complained with a little pout. She was cute and she knew how to play him. He was tempted to let her off any kind of punishment. Chase already had, once he saw what Col had done. Chase was still feeling guilty over having sold her information too, which didn't help.

"Well," he said, rubbing her pussy. "As long as you promise to be a very good girl."

"I'll be so good," she promised. "I'll do whatever you want!"

Col snorted and shook his head. "You spoil her."

"I'm allowed to spoil her," Max shot back. "She doesn't need five dudes destroying her." He looked down into Lacey's sweet face. "I forgive you, princess," he said. "I guess that just leaves Brian and Rex."

"Thank you!" Lacey wrapped her arms around his neck and kissed his cheek, her eyes shining with genuine gratitude. "Thank you so much, Max! I'm going to be so good, and I promise I'll make it up to you when the others are done with me."

"That's alright," he rumbled, patting her butt. "Just don't make a fool out of me again."

"He doesn't need any help," Col added.

CHAPTER TWENTY-ONE

Lacey
Three days later…

She'd received mercy from Chase and Max, but Brian had not revoked his right to punish her. Lacey was curious as to what he had in store for her. After Col, she wasn't actually afraid anymore. Nothing could be more intense than what Col had done, and Brian didn't show any signs of sadism, so she was confident the worst of the suffering was over.

He approached her one afternoon quite casually, almost as if the whole affair were a matter of second thought.

"Lacey, would you come out to the workshop with me?"

Brian smiled that elegant smile he had, the one that always made her blush. She was a different woman with each of the men. With Brian she felt like a lady, albeit a lady very much fallen from grace. This kindly invitation belied what he likely had in store for her.

"I've got something very special planned for you."

He took her by the hand and led her out to the workshop. She found herself smiling nervously. She hadn't spent as much time with Brian. He was more retiring than most, and he didn't inject himself into conversations unless he was asked to. She somewhat doubted he was upset with her the way Col and maybe Rex were. Rex had been distant, probably because he hadn't dealt with her yet. After Col, he was the one she was most worried about.

"Oh, my god!" A gasp escaped her as Brian conducted her into the workshop. He had prepared something very, very special.

It was the fucking machine—on steroids.

There were two dildo probes emanating from two long separate black shafts. There was a paddle attached to another arm and a little attachment for god knows what. A covered bench had been placed in front of the shafts and probes. Brian conducted her across to it and made a gesture like a waiter showing her to her table.

"Lie down, please."

Brian was always so polite. He was the most twisted of them all, but he didn't need to throw his weight around with overbearing machismo. She would have done as she was told out of curiosity. Settling face down on the bench, she found it pretty comfortable.

"Col took you in two places, but he's one man and he only has one cock," Brian declared. "This will allow me to take you in all three orifices."

"We haven't actually been together," she said, feeling a little shy.

Brian crouched down next to her and ran his long fingers through her hair, brushing it gently out of the way. "Does that bother you? I know you were upset about Chase not being intimate with you."

"I…" She shook her head. "I don't know. I just got used to your machines."

He flashed a handsome smile. "I think we have been together," he said. "I use my proxies, but I see your pleasure. You flush so beautifully, and I can keep you on the verge of climax so much longer."

"Aren't you supposed to be punishing me?"

"Maybe," he said with a wicked little grin. "We'll see how punished you feel. I'm going to strap you down so I can keep you in place and calibrate everything. Slide back for me a little more, knees on the floor, bottom off the edge of the bench."

She did as she was told, shimmying back into a position that left her rear fully accessible to Brian and to his machines. He grabbed a couple of small cushions for her knees and wrapped a big black leather strap over her back. The feeling of panic that usually accompanied being bound didn't rise at all. She relaxed against the bench with a deep sigh, giving in to what was about to happen.

Brian ran his hand over her bottom. "We should be together," he said. "Before the machines… I was worried about you, Lacey. But I know I'm the one who betrayed you."

"You were doing it on Rex's orders."

"Yes," he said, his fingers stroking lightly over her slit, parting her lower lips gently. "But I was the one who lied to your face." He inserted a finger inside her, slipping it deeply into her pussy and sliding it back out. She was wet. Had been almost perpetually since this punishment began. Col had ravaged her into a perpetual state of desire, and now as she was bound down against the bench, she felt herself leaking juices over Brian's finger.

"You did lie to me," she agreed, hissing softly as he took his finger away and replaced it with the smooth, hard head of his cock. Closing her eyes, she held her breath as he pushed in ever so slowly, spreading her pussy around his rod with a languid stroke that was utterly unhurried. Brian made love like a master, gently urging her cunt into submission. He stroked her back as he moved inside her, working his thick cock ever deeper.

"Oh, my god, Brian," she moaned softly. "This is… you're so… oh, my god…"

She could hear the soft wet sounds of her pussy. His cock was working back and forth inside her, urging her toward a glowing arousal that filled her entire body. Brian was the most patient of them all. He was the last one to make love to her, the last one to fill her with his flesh and as her toes curled, she realized she had been missing out.

Moaning his name over and over again, she squirmed her hips, working herself on him as much as she could. The leather strap prevented much movement though. He was squarely in control, keeping her pussy on a slow boil as he held himself still. She felt him reach around for something, and then a rounded surface found her clit. There was a clipping sound, as if it had been locked into place—and then it began to vibrate.

"Oooohhh, Briiaan!" she squealed as her pussy was flooded with pleasure. The toy was snug against her clit, the vibrations working through her lower flesh and taking her toward orgasm. "I'm going to come!"

"Good girl," Brian soothed. "Do it for me. Come on my cock, sweetheart."

She came obediently and immediately, her cunt clenching his cock as she felt her orgasm rush through her, spiraling along her spine and bursting into a bright cascade of pleasure that made her tingle all over, panting and writhing.

But he was still inside her, and the vibrator was still running. She was going to come again. She moaned and squirmed, but she couldn't escape and as Brian started to take her a little harder and faster, she started to come again. And again.

"Can I come inside you?" Brian panted the question as his cock swelled inside her.

"Yes!" she screamed. It was adorable that he asked, but there could only be one answer to the question. Yes. She needed his cum. Yes. She had to have him deeper inside her. Yes. Yes. A thousand times yes.

He let out a cry as he spent himself inside her, his cock plunging deep into her slippery slit, pumping his load inside her bare walls. And still it was not over, because the vibrator kept on vibrating and the additional wetness of cum and her own arousal slipping from her pussy down over her clit only served to heighten the pleasure. The tool got wetter and wetter, her pussy got more and more tender, but Brian was not done with her.

Where he ended, his machines began. Almost immediately he pushed the shaft with the dildo attached into her pussy. Again she was filled, moaning incoherently. He parted her cheeks, lubricated her tight little hole, and began to work the slightly smaller anal probe into place, pushing and twisting it with a screwing motion that inevitably made her flesh give way.

"Brian," she cried out. "I can't take any more."

"Yes, you can," he said calmly. "Your body is nice and lubricated, your sex is perfectly capable of taking much more stimulation, and your bottom is more receptive than I would have imagined too." Such clinical language, given he was talking about double fucking her with a sex machine.

Lacey lay there, racked with what now felt like almost continual orgasm as the probes started to push inside her, propelled by mechanical means that would not tire, or become flaccid, which would be able to keep filling both sensitive holes until the end of time. She was going to be fucked forever, her sweaty, writhing body caught in his instrument of pleasure torment.

"Brian, please… let me out. I can't take it…"

He walked around to face her, his nice smooth thick cock held in his hand. She saw how wet it still was with his cum and her juices. The sight almost set her off into another orgasm as he stepped forward and ran the head of his dick over her lips.

"You were a naughty girl," Brian lectured softly, pushing his cum-covered cock into her mouth. "I have to teach you a good long lesson so next time you don't do anything so foolish. You could have been hurt, Lacey, and that would have hurt all of us."

Lacey couldn't respond in any coherent way. She gasped

and panted around his cock, drooling desire over his dick as she cleaned it off, taking every little bit of his seed down her throat. By then she'd come at least ten times. Her thighs were weak and perpetually trembling, her pussy and ass felt as though they were being commercially used, the probes sliding in at slightly off phase intervals so the one in her ass would slide out just as the one in her pussy was sliding in.

"I know this is tough on you," Brian said sympathetically as she wailed her way through yet another climax. "But you have to learn."

"I've learned, Brian. I promise I have!"

He turned the vibrator off and stilled the probes. The one in her pussy had slipped free, but the one in her anus still had her stretched around it. He made no move to let her go. He kept her in position, her ass filled.

"What have you learned?" He asked the question gently and with real interest. Maybe he was a sadist. Maybe he was just a different kind of sadist.

"I know if I ever do anything like that again, I'm fucked. Literally."

He smiled a little. "Anything else?"

"I don't think so…"

Brian reached out to turn the machine back on.

"No!"

"You must have learned more than a glib one-liner," Brian encouraged. "Tell me. I want to know what you've learned. All of it."

"I've learned that I'm still in danger," she babbled hurriedly. "I've learned that if I act out, I put you in danger. I've learned that Col doesn't hate me, and you're not as innocent as you look. I've learned that Max is nicer than he seems and Chase still feels guilty and I don't know about Rex because he hasn't really talked to me in days."

Brian nodded and flipped a switch. The probe in her ass started to move, surging forward and then out of its own accord.

"I'll give your pussy a rest," he said. "But you haven't

taken much in your rear and I think you could do with some machine training."

"You're a sick puppy," she groaned as the dildo worked itself in and out of her ass, moving at a slow-ish pace, and doing just as Brian had said it would, making her ass relax so that it could move even more smoothly.

He grinned broadly. "I fit into this unit for a reason," he said. "I haven't played with you as much as I'd like, Lacey. When all this settles down, I have so many more machines to try on you."

Lacey grunted as the dildo in her ass went deep, stretching her hole wide before retreating yet again. She'd come so many times she didn't think it would be possible to come again, but something was building inside her. Something that arose from being strapped down and ass fucked by a machine while a handsome man told her of his plans for her. She was in very safe hands with him, and though he'd lied to her about the data, she found that she trusted him anyway. Brian's affection was twisted for sure, but so was hers.

"One more orgasm," he said, encouraging her. "One more big one. Show me what you've learned."

He turned the tempo of the machine up. Lacey grabbed the bench and squealed as the machine started to ram and rail her ass with quick, short strokes. Oh, fuck. She was going to come from being ass fucked by an inanimate object. She was going to come all over that thing, and she was going to do it under the watchful gaze of a man who engineered pleasure and pain to perfection.

Just when she thought she was about to come, he activated the final piece of the puzzle: the spanking machine. The paddle rotated around and caught her ass with a solid whack that made her jolt against her bindings.

Whap!

"Ow!"

"I know you can come while you're being punished," Brian crooned. "So do it. Let the pain make you feel better."

Whap!

The paddle landed again, stinging her ass terribly. She let out a shriek, but there was no quarter to be given, not from the dildo in her rear and not from the paddle itself. Lacey lay there, writhing in her bonds, her ass fucked and punished more thoroughly by Brian than by anyone. She stared at him in shock as the paddle made another rotation, searing her already tender skin.

Whap!

The sensations were building in her already orgasm-fatigued body. Coming wasn't as simple without stimulation against her clit or in her pussy. All she had now was the pain and the pounding of her ass… and Brian. Looking into those green eyes of his, she found herself flooded with heat. He was possibly the most dangerous of all of them, the youngest of the lot and by far the most devious. He had lulled her into a false sense of security, stolen her data, come in her pussy, and now he was tormenting her in ways Col couldn't even begin to dream of.

"What have you learned, Lacey?"

"Not to fuck with you," she gasped.

He smiled broadly and flicked the vibrator on again. The burst of sensation sent her over the edge immediately, making her convulse as the most powerful orgasm yet slammed through her body, every part of her flesh alight with desire as she screamed her release to the world. She could hardly breathe, she couldn't see. Everything was bright and then it was dark and her body was trembling from head to toe as she shivered and writhed, whimpering for mercy as the waves began to recede and the vibrations became more uncomfortable than anything else.

"Shhh, good girl," Brian said, finally turning the machine off completely. "We're done, for now."

"For now?" She asked the question weakly.

"Mhm," Brian pressed an almost chaste kiss to her forehead as she lay there bound and desperate, her ass and pussy dripping with lubricant, semen, and her shameful feminine reaction to his sadistic punishment.

• • • • • • •

Two days later…

She was exhausted, but she was also almost done. There was just one man to go. It had taken several days to recover from Brian's punishment, physically and mentally. He had taken her to places she hadn't known it was possible to go. He had shown her the limits of her body's orgasmic response, and shown her that in surrender there was more pleasure than she could imagine. He had also shown her that the same pleasure could be turned against her and used as a weapon of strict discipline.

She looked at him differently now. He no longer seemed like the shy little guy of the group. He was the dark horse, the one it was all too easy to underestimate. She'd never do that again.

"Are you alright?" Brian slid up to her with a small smile.

"Yeah," she said, wrapping her blanket around her. "Just hoping to get this stuff with Rex over so I can get some new clothes. Kinda tired of running around naked all the time."

"Well, why don't you go see him? I think he's in his room."

She was nervous to go and see Rex. The leader of the pack had been aloof to the extreme since the incident. Lacey felt closer to everyone else than ever before, but he had absolutely pulled away, both from her, and by proxy, the rest of the group. He was quite often removed from the men, preferring to read in his office rather than socialize with them.

"I think he hates me," she said softly.

Brian glanced in the general direction of Rex's room, his eyes squinting a bit almost as if he was trying to see through the walls.

"He doesn't like being defied," Brian said. "And you

really defied him. I don't think he knows what to do with you."

"He always knows everything."

"Maybe not this. If I were you I'd go and apologize."

CHAPTER TWENTY-TWO

Rex

A small knock at Rex's door heralded the conversation he'd been avoiding having for a week. The boys had done an incredible job of bringing Lacey to justice for her actions. Rex was actually quite proud of them. But he was troubled too. It was one thing to punish her, but he had to be sure that the punishment would actually do something—and he wasn't certain that it would. Lacey wasn't the type to roll over and submit. She was strong minded and brave. And that made her a serious problem for him. They could spank her all they wanted, but when she got another idea in her head she'd be off to follow it and damn the consequences. It was just who she was.

"Come in." He closed his book and sat up in his chair, waiting for her to enter.

She crept into the room, swaddled in a blanket. She wasn't supposed to have any clothes, but it was a colder day and rules didn't really apply to her anyway, apparently. At least she hadn't managed to charm one of the others into going and buying her a new wardrobe yet.

"What is it, Lacey?"

"I'm sorry," she said, looking down at her hands. "I shouldn't have taken the van, and I shouldn't have gone to the media. It was a mistake."

Rex rubbed his hand over his jaw and looked at her grimly. Mistake was an understatement.

"I know you're upset at me," she continued, her voice small and wavering. "And I know it's different for you."

"What do you mean?"

She shifted nervously. "I mean, Chase and Max felt sorry for me and Col and Brian punished me, but it's different for you. I didn't really do anything to them directly. I mean, I did, but…" She looked up at him. "You're in charge of us all, so when one of us does something wrong, it's kind of… I don't know how to say it… worse for you."

Maybe she did understand the problem. Or maybe one of the guys had explained it to her. That was a start, but it wasn't enough.

"It's a problem, Lacey."

Her face fell. "I know, I'm sorry."

"Are you?"

"Yes! If you'd seen what I've let them do to me to make up for this…"

"It's not about making up for," Rex said. "It's about the discipline we live by. I have four strong-willed, intelligent, dangerous men out there. If they did whatever they felt like doing, this unit would fall apart in two seconds. They don't do as I say because they don't have their own minds, or because they always agree with me. They do it because they know this is the only way we can work together, stay together. So when you disregard my orders and go running across the country to yap on television, it's not just that you defy me, it's that you undermine everything we believe in. How can we keep you with us when we can't trust you? We can't constantly be on guard against you and what you might do. We can't lock every door, hide every key. Not forever."

"I know. And you don't have to. I won't do anything that stupid again, I promise. I learned my lesson."

"Did you?"

"Yes," she said, her eyes wide and earnest. "Please, Rex, sir, you have to believe me."

He didn't believe her. That was the problem.

"Just punish me, please," she whimpered. "I'll show you."

"What would punishing you do? Discipline only works when you care about not wanting to be disciplined again. But you crave it, Lacey. You like pain. You like trouble. And that's cute for five minutes, but it doesn't work long term."

Her lower lip quivered. "I'm sorry," she said, sounding heartbroken.

"So am I."

"So what are you saying? Do you want me to leave?"

Rex shook his head. "I haven't decided what to do with you yet."

She bit her lower lip. "Well, I've kept my side of the deal, so if it's okay with you, I'd like to get some clothes, and I'm going to need some, er, feminine products."

"Get one of the guys to take you out," Rex said. "It's fine."

Lacey looked like she was going to burst into tears. "Please… Rex… I am sorry, really I am. And you did betray me…"

"Betray you?" He growled the words. "I did what I thought was best. I told you what you needed to know. If you had just kept your nose out of things, we would have saved ourselves a lot of time and trouble. As it is, I'm getting report after report of Fishland's people looking for you. That visit to the TV studio put them on edge. You're in more danger now than you ever have been."

"I didn't know that…"

"No. Because you didn't need to, or at least, I didn't think you did."

"They still want me dead? What about the CIA?"

"They haven't acted on the material yet."

"I knew they wouldn't," Lacey scowled. "I told you…"

"No," he snapped coldly. "You don't tell me anything. You are the one who gets told. Get out of here before I whip your ass."

Rex was furious. He wanted to take off his belt and lash her butt until she cried, but he was too damn angry to punish her right now. He understood Col now. The girl really had a way of getting under his skin, a combination of submission and rebellion that just didn't work.

Lacey's face turned red and she made a half turn before pivoting back to him. She opened her mouth…

"Go!" Rex thundered the word at her.

She fled.

CHAPTER TWENTY-THREE

Lacey

"He hates me," she sniveled against Chase's chest. "He really, really hates me."

"He doesn't hate you," Chase soothed her, running his hand over her hair. "He's just really not good with women and even worse with disobedience. He was a hard ass when we were in the service, and he hasn't changed much since then."

"He doesn't want me to be here anymore. He wants to get rid of me. He's going to send me away," Lacey sobbed, totally miserable. Rex had been fucking terrifying when he yelled at her. She hadn't expected him to be so angry. It had been over a week since she'd run off, and he didn't seem to be getting over it at all. He'd screamed at her like he was a drill sergeant and she was some unruly soldier, and it had left her shaken.

"If he wanted to send you away, you'd be gone," Chase said. "Besides, that ship has sailed. You're ours now. Part of the team. Even Col has come around to that. Rex knows he'd have a mutiny on his hands if he tried to get rid of you now."

"So he doesn't want me, but he has to keep me," she sniffed. "That's even worse."

"I'm sure he wants you," Chase soothed. "Give him time, and some space."

Just then, there was a tap at the door. "Is Lacey in there?"

"Yeah, she's here," Chase said, easing her up from his chest. Lacey looked around to see Max standing in the doorway.

"Come on," Max said, jingling the keys. "I'm taking you for ice cream."

"And tampons."

He made a grimace. "I don't think they go well together."

"You're so dumb," Lacey laughed.

"And clothes," he added. "It's about time you got something that fits you. Can't wear Chase's castoffs forever."

"Are you coming?" She looked back at Chase.

"I've got some work to do here. You and Max have a fun girl's trip."

Max twirled his hair and gave a faux giggle, making Lacey laugh. Rex might be crazy, but she loved these men so much. She wasn't going to leave them, not for anything.

CHAPTER TWENTY-FOUR

Rex

"I got Max to take Lacey out, because we need to discuss this situation," Rex said. He'd assembled his remaining men into the living room: Col, Chase, and Brian. None of them were going to be on board with his upcoming suggestion, but they had to have this discussion regardless.

"Try to put aside your personal feelings for a moment and look at this situation objectively. We have a target we're trying to protect, one who doesn't want to be protected half the time and who is reckless enough to put herself in danger at any moment. Lacey is unpredictable. I don't trust her."

"She's a pain in the ass," Col agreed. "She's reckless and undisciplined and she makes terrible decisions. But she can be taught."

"I don't think so," Rex said. "We're going to have to make a lot of decisions she doesn't like over time. If she steals our things and runs away every time, it's dangerous for her and for us. She's a grown woman, and I reckon it's too late to change her. She wasn't trustworthy when we met her, and she's not trustworthy now. You boys have put the work in on her, but I'm still not convinced. She was prepared to argue with me even after everything you did. That tells me she hasn't learned much, if anything."

"She hasn't had enough time," Brian interjected. "Discipline and obedience take time to instill. Especially in women."

Rex looked at Chase, who shook his head. "You may be right. I think she'd be better away from this kind of environment. It doesn't suit her."

It was upside down day. It had to be. Col was arguing for Lacey, and Chase was saying she might be an ongoing issue.

"Why?"

"I'd go with her," Chase said, suddenly making a lot more sense. "Make sure she doesn't get into trouble."

"You just want her to yourself," Col said bluntly.

Chase looked over at him, his eyes narrowed. "I actually want what's best for her. And that isn't being constantly whipped and tied and put away. She deserves a real life. A house. A family."

"Chase wants to marry her and knock her up and play tea parties," Col snorted. "God, you don't know her at all. She'd go crazy in that kind of life. And she'd drive you crazy too. You couldn't handle her on your own. None of us could. Hell, she's already broken Rex."

"What's that supposed to mean," Rex growled.

"You've been sulking," Col said. "Should have just fucked her ass nice and hard and taught her a lesson, but instead you've been moping around refusing to talk to her. As if she cares. She survived weeks of militia torture. Your silent treatment isn't going to do shit to her."

"The van's back," Brian said softly.

They all fell silent as Max and Lacey returned and came inside. Lacey was dressed in a pair of jeans and a sweatshirt that actually fit her. It was sort of weird to see her dressed semi-normally. To Rex's relief she shuffled off quickly toward the bedrooms, leaving Max standing in the living room, giving them all a quizzical look.

"What are you talking about?" Max inquired.

"I was just saying Rex should punish Lacey and get it over with," Col said, "'cause the silent treatment doesn't affect her. "

"I don't know about that," Brian interjected. "I think she's pretty nervous. She keeps being sick."

"Being sick?" Rex raised a brow. "What do you mean? Food poisoning?"

"I dunno. She was sick the other morning with me."

"Yeah, yesterday with me too," Max agreed. "But I think it's just her period. She got some girl stuff today."

"Girl stuff?"

"You know, period stuff. I don't know. I let her get whatever she wanted. I wasn't looking."

"You weren't looking!" Rex nearly exploded. "You just let her wander around in a store by herself?"

"I don't know what girls need. She just grabbed a few things. She didn't attempt to take down a shadowy cabal or anything."

"You let her loose in a fucking pharmacy. She could have gotten anything!"

"You want to check her tampons? Check her tampons," Max snorted. "I wasn't going to get into it."

"She's not bleeding though," Col said. "I was with her last night."

"They don't bleed constantly, do they?" Brian spoke up. "Maybe she was in a non-bleeding part of it."

Rex palmed his face. Five military men attempting to unravel the mystery of their captive's menstrual cycle was ridiculous.

"Does it matter? We're dealing with an ongoing security risk. We can't trust her, and frankly, I don't see how we ever will."

"But we took her on," Max said. "You can't take a woman and get rid of her just because she's trouble. There's five of us and one of her. You're just mad because she defied you. You should work it out with her."

How was he supposed to work it out? Lacey was uncontrollable. She didn't believe in loyalty. She didn't believe in obedience. She didn't believe in anything besides the next story, and sooner or later, she was going to go off in search of it.

Rex was worried for his men. He'd thought that they were the ones taking Lacey, but in reality, Lacey had stolen all of their hearts. Yes, even his. He loved the little spitfire, but he didn't see how she could ever be contained.

At practically the worst moment possible, he heard her voice coming from behind him.

"Uhm… guys? I need to talk to you."

"Fine, come in," Rex sighed. She may as well be present for the conversation. Maybe they'd get somewhere with her in the room. Maybe not.

She did look pale and exhausted, he admitted to himself. She didn't meet his eye, or actually, any of their gazes. She was twisting something between her hands, something long and pale-looking. Toothbrush shiv?

"I don't know how to say this, so I'll just show you."

She put the slim panel of plastic down on the coffee table. Immediately, everyone started to talk over one another.

"What is that?"

"Is that a travel toothbrush?"

"It's a pregnancy test, idiot."

Lacey put their questions to rest with a simple statement. "It's positive. I'm pregnant."

The silence in the room was complete as all five men stared at that little blue plus sign.

Rex racked his brains. It couldn't be his. He was fixed. Unless his vasectomy had failed, but that wasn't likely. But it could belong to literally any one of the others. Every single one of them had been with her. Every single one of them should have known better than to come inside her, but Rex hadn't been there to slap the dicks out of her pussy before they came.

"Damn," Col said under his breath.

"Wow," Chase agreed.

Brian looked like he'd stopped breathing entirely. Max's deer in the headlights expression also showed a lack of immediate joy at the revelation. That plastic stick had turned the room into a game of statue. Nobody knew what to say or to do. Was this cause for celebration? Even Lacey didn't look as though she knew.

"What do you want to do?" Rex turned to Lacey. It was her body. It was her choice. If he understood correctly, she wasn't all that far along and he wasn't so naive as to think every woman in the universe wanted to be a mother. Especially not ones like Lacey.

"You mean…" she put her hand over her belly, "you mean do I want this?"

"Yes."

She looked at him. "Do you?"

Rex drew in a breath. "We don't know who the father is, but I know it's not me. So I'm the last person you should be asking."

"I'm not asking who the father is. I'm asking you," she said. "You. Personally. You. Do you want me?"

"What does that have to do…"

"Tell me, Rex." Tears glimmered in her eyes. "Do you want me gone? Because I'll go. I'll leave you all. I know this wasn't in the plan. You wanted revenge on me, not to knock me up and play happy families with me. So I'll go and make your lives easier."

She was hormonal. Emotional. And she wasn't going any-damn-where.

"You're still mine," he said. "You're still ours. But none of us are going to make this choice for you."

"I want it," she said softly. "But I don't know how I'm going to do it. It can't live in a cabin in the woods forever. It can't hide from snipers. It can't have five dads."

"Why not?" Max spoke up.

"What?"

"Why can't it have five dads? Why can't we live in the woods?"

Rex figured Max hadn't addressed the part about snipers, because she had a good point. Senator Fishland was still on the warpath. The CIA hadn't acted, and may never act. That meant her life was still in danger. And it meant the life inside her was in danger too. That fact didn't have to be spoken out loud. Everyone understood it.

"I can't have this," she said, her eyes filled with the most tragic tears Rex had ever seen. "I can't bring a baby into this. It's better just to have a…"

Col got up and grabbed her tight before she could finish her sentence. "It's going to be okay," he growled. "You're going to be okay, the baby is going to be okay. We're going to make damn sure of it. Trust me."

Rex looked on, his expression impassive as a whirlwind of emotions rushed through him. This situation had just gotten even more grave, and a lot of options had just been put right off the table. The boys were right. Sending her away wasn't an option, and never should have crossed his mind. She was trouble, but she was their trouble—and he was going to stop sulking and start doing what he damn well needed to do.

CHAPTER TWENTY-FIVE

Lacey

Lacey was shattered. This was about the very last thing she had planned on, though she had known it was a possibility being with so many men. Maybe even more of an inevitability. Still, for it to happen this quickly? That was some timing. Some fucking horrible timing.

Col was the last person she'd expected to comfort her first, but he was always full of surprises. He held her so tight and spoke with such conviction that she almost believed him. Chase was the next to grab her, joining in to make it a double hug.

"We want this. We want you," he said. "And heaven help anyone who tries to hurt either one of you."

"Max? Brian?" She looked at them both with tears swimming in her eyes.

"You've got us, girl," Max rumbled.

Brian just smiled. It was all she needed. They were on board. She had four of them, and four mercenaries were a lot more than most babies had to keep them safe. Maybe this would work after all. She still didn't see how, but she had faith in her men.

"Go lie down," Chase said gently. "We're going to need to talk. Dad stuff."

She gave a little smile. "I'd like to hear whatever dad stuff gets discussed."

"Not this stuff," he said firmly. "And I know you're tired. You need a nap…"

"I'll take her," Rex said, surprising her. "Lacey and I have a reckoning to come."

"We're going to have to make some decisions, Rex," Chase said, his voice somewhat tense. There was something behind his eyes. Something Lacey didn't quite like. It was a look she hadn't seen before, a darkness and a determination that didn't seem directed at her, but had to be connected.

"I know," Rex replied. "You've got full authorization to make them. You boys know what you're doing, and what has to be done."

The others nodded.

"What are you talking about?" Something was going on again. Something she didn't understand. She was distracted by the conversation she was being cut out of by the fact that Rex suddenly seemed willing to speak to her. His entire demeanor had changed. He wasn't cold anymore, but he was still stern as he looked down at her and took her by the hand.

"The boys are right," he said. "I need to deal with you. Come on, little girl."

Little girl. She could have cried at hearing him call her that again. With her head spinning, she followed Rex down to his room, her hand tucked in his. He took her into his room, shut the door behind her, and lightly swatted her further into the room.

Lacey yelped and skipped forward, her hands over her rear as she turned to face him.

"So you've gotten yourself knocked up," he drawled.

"Yes… Daddy." She used the word nervously, worried that he would reject her for it. He didn't. He smiled, his handsome face lighting up in a way that made her squirm deep in her belly. Rex was so handsome. His gravitas and strong features, that salt and pepper hair that marked him as the silverback, it all reinforced the man he was, and her reaction was a sign of just how much she needed him and his approval.

"Well," he said. "That's one way to slow you down."

"Yeah," she agreed, somewhat ruefully. "I'm going to get big."

"Uh huh, and you're going to have someone depending on you. Someone who will need you to be there for them to keep them safe. The stakes just got raised, Lacey, big time. It's not just about you anymore."

"I know," she said, even though she wasn't really sure she did. She hadn't ever imagined she'd be a mother, much less under circumstances like these. "I'm in trouble, aren't I."

"Mhm. You're in some kind of trouble. It's going to be up to you to decide what kind it is. Either you're in the kind of trouble where you settle down and become a good mother and have us look after you, or you're in the kind of trouble where real tragedies happen."

"I'm not going to let anything happen to my baby."

My baby. The words sounded foreign. It was strange, but the moment she'd seen that blue plus sign, she'd become someone new. Was that even possible? Could your world shift in an instant? It had before, first when she was taken in Venezuela, then when Rex and his men had taken her. Why not again? There was a life inside her. A life that didn't deserve to be born into chaos and pain.

"Neither are we," Rex growled softly. "Don't worry about that."

Lacey smiled with pure relief. "I thought you'd be so angry about this. I thought you'd hate me for getting pregnant."

"It's not as though you have control over it," he said. "My men did though, and I'm betting by their reactions each and every one of them put you in the position to be a mother."

"Yes," she admitted softly, feeling a little embarrassed. Rex had been the first to have sex with her, so why was she so nervous to admit she'd been with the others? He confused her in so many ways. He felt paternal and yet she was deeply attracted to him. When there was trouble, she was always most in trouble with him. He was the center of things.

"You've been a very bad girl for Daddy, haven't you."

"Yes," she admitted with a little sob. His words were such a relief. She loved it when he played along with the daddy thing. It served to satisfy some need inside her, some place none of her needs had ever been satisfied. "I'm sorry, Daddy."

Rex sat back in an armchair that was near the bed. It was broad enough that almost two people could fit on it, but he sat dead in the center. She watched as he slid his fly down, his cock springing out already fully erect.

"Get those clothes off and get your pussy over here," he growled softly.

Lacey didn't waste time disobeying him. She pulled her clothes off and left them in a pile on the floor then walked to him, feeling shy and aroused at the same time. She'd thought that he'd never want to be with her again, but his thick erection said otherwise.

He reached out, his large hands finding her bottom as he pulled her forward and into a kneeling straddling position over him.

"Show your daddy just how sorry you are," he murmured, rubbing her bottom in slow circles.

Lacey did not need to be told twice. She lowered herself obediently onto his dick, her slippery wet slit taking him deep.

"That's right," he groaned. "Take it deep, girl, work that naughty cunt."

She moaned as she worked herself on his dick, obediently pleasuring her daddy. The look in Rex's eyes was one of steely passion as he reached out, gripped her by the hips and held her down on his dick, making her take the full length of it.

"Tell me something, Lacey."

"Yes, Daddy?"

"You know better than to let men come inside this hot slippery little cunt of yours, don't you?"

"Yes," she blushed.

"And yet you let them do it, didn't you. How many of them could be the father, girl?"

"Uhm." She squirmed on his cock. "Well, uhh…"

He slapped her bottom. "Tell me honestly."

"Chase and Col and Brian," she gasped.

"You let three men come inside your pussy?"

"Yes, Daddy."

Really, it could only be one man. Col and Brian had been too recent for her to test positive from their couplings.

"You know whose it is though, don't you."

"Uhm, I think so."

Rex lifted her up and down on his cock in a slow thrust. "It's Chase, isn't it."

"Yes, Daddy," she moaned as Rex used her.

"Mhm. I thought so. You've been craving his cum for a long time, haven't you."

"Yes," she admitted as he ground her down on his dick.

"I bet you begged him to come inside your naughty pussy, knowing exactly what would happen. Is that what you did, my girl? Did you ask Chase to fuck you bare and fill you up with his cum?"

Again she had to say yes. Again he spanked her bottom.

"You've been a very, very, naughty girl," he lectured. "I don't know that I can trust you out of my sight. I think I might have to keep your pussy locked up."

"Too late, Daddy," she giggled. "Ow!"

His hand met her bottom again as he pulled her down against his chest, kept his cock locked inside her and started to spank her properly, her poor bare cheeks spread over his lap, vulnerable to each and every stroke of his hard hand.

Rex used her while he punished her, her cunt clenching his cock with every slap until he came inside her, still spanking her through his orgasm, whipping her bottom harder and harder as he shot his seed deep inside her bare cunt.

"Fuck that cum into you," he ordered. "Bounce on my cock, girl."

Lacey obeyed, working her ass up and down his hard shaft while he kept spanking her.

"Look at that cum slipping out of you," he lectured. "Such a sloppy girl."

His lecturing and his spanking and the cum making her clit nice and slippery soon started to tip Lacey toward her own climax. She had needed this with Rex for so long. She wrapped her arms around his neck and cuddled into him as she rocked her ass back and forth, riding his cock with her wet pussy.

"Thank you, Daddy," she gasped into his ear as she started to come, her orgasm rushing through her body, giving her the relief she had needed for so long. She needed Rex's approval. She didn't quite know why, but she knew she did. Nothing felt right if he wasn't pleased with her.

"You're welcome, little girl," he murmured, holding her close, keeping her on his cock.

"Am I forgiven?"

"Yes," he said, running his hand up and down her back. "You're forgiven. I'm going to be here for you, Lacey, for you and this baby for as long as you need me."

"That's going to be forever."

He smiled down at her and kissed her cheek. "Forever it is."

CHAPTER TWENTY-SIX

Lacey

"Chase," Lacey murmured under her breath as she cuddled with him in the kitchen. "Is it okay if the baby is yours?"

"It's okay," he purred back. "Because that baby is going to be mine no matter what. Just like you're going to be mine, no matter what."

"And the others? What about them? Do you think they'll lose interest in me now?"

That had been worrying her. She loved this arrangement, but if Chase was the father of the baby, and the others felt like they weren't part of her life anymore, she could see a future where they all drifted apart. That made her sad to think about. She wanted all of her men forever, greedy as that sounded in her own mind.

"We all have claim to you," Chase said. "We all have our different connections, different needs. You're something different for each and every one of us. I don't think anyone is losing interest in you."

Lacey wasn't so sure. Since they found out she was pregnant, most of the others had been around a lot less.

They said they had work to do, but she felt like they were avoiding her. Right now, Max and Col and Brian were all gone. They'd headed out a day or so earlier and hadn't even said goodbye. She'd been sleeping when they left, and when she woke to discover them missing, she had worried. Chase and Rex had made plenty of plausible noises about their whereabouts, but Lacey could tell something was happening. Her journalist senses were tingling.

"They're due back really soon, I think," Chase said. "Why don't you watch some TV."

She may as well, she figured. There was nothing else to do. Being holed up and hiding from assassins while pregnant was not as much fun as it sounded, and it didn't sound like any fun in the first place.

Lacey wandered into the living room, curled up on the couch, and turned the TV on.

Breaking news: Senator Fishland found dead at his home in what appears to be an accidental death.

"Holy…" She sat up, her eyes wide. "Chase! Look at this! He's dead! The fucker's dead!"

Chase didn't look as surprised as she thought he should. "That was quick."

"What was quick? He's dead. And an accident at home, how's that for poetic justice. Karma!"

"Col, more likely."

"What?" Lacey turned around and stared at Chase. His comment didn't seem lighthearted. It seemed serious. "Is that… are they… did…" She lowered her voice to a hushed whisper. "They couldn't…"

At that exact moment, the van came rumbling up the drive. Lacey abandoned the couch and ran out to meet Col and Max and Brian, all of whom disembarked looking tired and a little worse for wear.

"Where have you been?"

Max scooped her up into a hug. "We went for ice cream," he lied. "It was so good we ate it all so we couldn't bring you any."

"I just saw the news," she said. "Fishland is dead?" She knew better than to ask the follow-up question as they looked at her with those practiced military expressions. The ones that gave absolutely nothing away. Max was still holding her, so she actually looked down on them for once, albeit over his shoulder.

"The baby is going to be safe," Col said, indirectly answering the question that had gone unasked. "And so are you."

"But the CIA said they were going to monitor the situation. They said it could be years…" Lacey stared at them. In her association with them they had been antagonists, lovers, playmates, and more but in this moment they were what they truly were for themselves. Mercenaries. Killers. And they'd just taken out a senator on her baby's behalf.

That was fucking bad ass.

CHAPTER TWENTY-SEVEN

Rex
Six months later...

Pregnancy was the best thing that could ever have happened to Lacey, as well as to Rex and his men. From the moment she'd shown them that pregnancy test, their priorities had changed. Matters had been dealt with. The senator had gotten what was coming to him after they'd done what they really should have done in the first place. None of them took assassination lightly, but if there was ever an asshole who deserved a bullet, it was Fishland. The truth was his days had been numbered from the moment they took her in. The continued threat to Lacey's life could not and would not have been tolerated much longer, but that little blue cross had brought matters to a head.

Rex hadn't realized when they first made their bargain to protect her that they would fall in love with Lacey. He'd known Chase was sweet on her, but he had never anticipated the deeper feelings that had grown between all of them. He hadn't even realized how much he loved her himself until he was faced first with the consequences of her insubordination and then the unprotected sex she'd been having.

He loved that girl in a way he hadn't known it was possible to love a woman, and though he'd never wanted any offspring of his own, this was different. Chase was going to be a great dad, and Rex could already see Col and Max taking an interest they hadn't before. Brian was a little more quiet about things, but even he seemed pleased. As a unit they'd been through several big transitions. Adjusting to fatherhood was the biggest one yet.

He was going to be responsible for five men, one woman, and an infant—and he couldn't wait.

• • • • • • •

Lacey

Pregnancy was the worst thing that could have happened to Lacey.

She was swollen, she was miserable, and there was little any of the men could do about it. Brian had taken to hiding out in the shed most of the time as she went on what they were starting to call her rampages. They weren't entirely her fault. The hormones were hard to control, and she barely recognized her body these days. Her ankles were swollen, her appetite was out of control, and she occasionally got kicked in the liver. Most of the men were unsympathetic to her plight. They didn't understand what it was like to have their bodies play host to new life. They seemed perplexed at her mood swings, and preferred to keep out of her way as she patrolled the house like an angry lioness looking for prey.

On a pass of the lounge, she caught Max and Col joking about drawing straws for who would give the other one a DIY home vasectomy first.

"This must never happen again," Col said, not quite out of earshot. "She could decimate a small nation with that gas."

"The gas is nothing," Max replied. "I forgot to put the cap on the toothpaste and she almost put a cap in my ass."

"Well, maybe you should remember simple things!" Lacey flared at them. "And don't act like me being pregnant is hard on you. You're not the one with a human inside you."

"Whoa, easy, Momma." Max put his hands up. "Don't deploy your biological weapons."

"Oh, fuck…"

"That's enough, Lacey." Rex's voice came from behind her. "You can settle down now. I don't care what state you're in, I'll find a way to discipline you if I need to."

"Did you hear what they were fucking saying about me?" She scowled at Rex. He was about the only one of the group willing to stand up to her in her current state, and secretly she was glad for it, though she hadn't admitted it, and likely never would.

"Swear at me again and you'll have your mouth washed out," Rex growled.

She hated being pregnant. She felt as though pregnancy had taken her men away from her and left her helpless. She was useless to herself and to everyone else and now that she was showing, the raucous sex that had started to taper off as soon as she told them the news had abated entirely and in its place was nothing but treatment with kid gloves.

Lacey was tired of it. She was tired of being a big blubbery waddling whale who never got laid. She was tired of being kicked from the inside out. She was tired of pretty much everything.

"Wash my mouth out and I'll get my revenge," she threatened Rex.

"Oh, yes, little girl?"

"Yeah, so don't fucking try it."

It turned out that pregnant women could be taken by the ear and waddle-marched to the bathroom. It also turned out that pregnant women could have bars of soap pushed into their mouths even as they made dire threats of what they'd do if that happened.

Spluttering on bitter soap, Lacey spat the bar out into the sink and gave Rex a foamy glare. "You can't do that! Soap's not safe!"

"It's perfectly safe," he growled. "What's not safe is you antagonizing everybody. You're about to be sent to your room, young lady. Is that what you want?"

She softened a little as Rex glowered sternly at her.

"No," she said in a small voice. "I want this baby out of me."

"Soon," he said.

"But it's not soon. It's three months. It's ninety days of having someone shank me in the bladder."

"The baby doesn't have a shank."

"I'm pretty sure he's turned part of the umbilical cord into a shiv," she rumbled, bending down to rinse her mouth of the bitter soap taste.

Rex watched her, his lips curling up into a smile.

"What's so funny?"

"You're going to look back on these as some of the best days of your life," he said. "You're going to remember being tucked up here in a cabin with all of us. This is the part before the happily ever after, little girl. It's coming. You just have to wait a little longer."

Lacey felt tears rising to her eyes. Her happily ever after was already here as far as she was concerned. She grabbed Rex and hugged him as best she could, shedding happy hormonal tears on his chest as he held her tight.

CHAPTER TWENTY-EIGHT

Lacey
Three months later...

"I am not going into labor without them here."

Lacey had been in labor for hours already, but she wasn't ready to have the baby. Rex had insisted on taking her to the hospital just because the contractions were three minutes apart, but Lacey was determined not to have the baby until everyone was with her. Chase and Rex were in the room, but the other three were AWOL, and that was not good enough. She had been very specific that everybody had to be there.

"Lacey, that's not how this works," Chase said soothingly. "When your body is ready, it's ready."

"Yes, it is. I will bake this baby until it is ready to go to college if I have to," she growled. "I want them here... ooowwwwww."

A tightening from the back of her spine all the way around to her belly began again. A contraction. She didn't want a contraction. She didn't want to do this. It was going to hurt worse than anything had ever hurt. She'd made the mistake of watching a bunch of birth videos and had come to the conclusion that the scene from *Alien* was less disturbing.

"Breathe," Chase soothed.

"I'm fucking breathing," Lacey snapped back. She was on hands and knees, panting like an animal. "Go and get them."

"I can't just go and get them, Lacey."

"They said they'd be here."

"They said they would try to," Chase said. "They didn't know you'd be going into labor today."

"Aarrggghhhh…" Lacey screamed as another contraction made everything horribly tight and painful again. "Get them now!"

"Easy, girl," Rex growled. He was not taking her shit no matter how far she was dilated, which at that point was eight centimeters.

"What? What are you going to do to me? I'm in labor, bitch!"

"You're not going to be in labor forever," Rex growled. "And I'll remember that."

"I am going to be in labor forever," she snapped back. "I've been in labor forever and I'm going to be in labor forever. This is never, ever going to end."

"Shhh," Chase soothed, wiping her forehead with a damp cloth. "Do you want some more ice chips?"

"I want throwing stars," she grunted. "And you can shove them up your ass and see how this feels… owww goddammmnnitt!"

Another contraction hit her like a freight train.

"You planned this all along, didn't you," she growled at Chase when she regained the ability to speak. "You knew if you knocked me up I'd suffer."

"Did we miss anything?" Max came striding through the door, oblivious as all hell. He was followed by Col and Brian.

"Do you see a baby?" Col interjected.

Max's reply was cut off by the arrival of the midwife, back to check her cervix. She pushed her hand under the blanket and glanced up at Lacey.

"You want all five of them here?"

"Yes, they're all the father. They've been drawing straws to see who gets to name the baby," Lacey said, enjoying the look of barely repressed shock on the woman's face.

"Alright then," she said with a smile. "You're ten centimeters. It's time to push."

"Hell, yeah," Max championed. "Time to push! Shoot that sucker out of there! We'll be home for tea."

"That's not how this works," the midwife said. "It takes time."

"How much time?"

"She's a new mother, so it could be a while. Her body needs to work out what it's doing."

"Oh," Max said with a small frown. "It doesn't know?"

"You're sure you want him here?" The midwife checked with Lacey again.

"Definitely," Lacey smiled. Max would be a distraction from everything that was to come. As her labor progressed, all the men settled into watchful vigil. Brian pressed a kiss to her forehead then sat down in the corner of the room and went to work on his laptop. Max stood there looking confused and out of place. Col was hovering near the door, a sort of angry expression on his face, which she now knew didn't actually mean he was angry. Col was a hammer and every problem that wasn't a nail bothered him. He was worried for her and he wanted to fight something, but there was nothing to fight. Just his presence made her feel better.

"Okay," she breathed. "Now I can do this."

Over the next three hours, she reneged on that point of view. She couldn't do this. It didn't make sense. Babies couldn't come out of people, the math didn't work out. The baby was too big. She was too small. Everything was stretching, there was tearing and blood and chaos.

Max went to have a look at how things were progressing and promptly fainted. He had to be carried out by Brian and Rex while Col and Chase talked her through it, mostly telling her to breathe, which was stupid as hell because telling someone who had a person coming out of her to breathe was a lot like telling a dude getting his eyes gouged out to remember to breathe. It was the least of her concerns, to say the least.

Finally, somewhere in the midst of the pressure and the pushing and the ongoing reminders to keep metabolizing oxygen, a thin cry heralded the birth of her son. She could hardly believe it when the midwife took him and put him on her chest. He was so tiny, so perfectly formed. She stared at the little face and felt a rush of love like no other. It was so hard to believe that he had been growing inside her all this time and now he was here, with her.

"He's beautiful," Chase breathed, pressing a kiss to her forehead.

Rex didn't say anything, but she saw the look of pride glimmering in his eyes, which he would have sworn up and down were not filled with tears.

Max returned to the room and crowded around. "Cool," he said enthusiastically. "He looks like Chase… or maybe Col… or Brian… or…"

"He looks like all of us because babies don't look like anything," Col said. "He looks like a potato."

"Col!" Rex snapped sharply.

"It's true," Col shrugged, rolling his eyes. "Okay, fine, he's cute. Whatever." He extended his finger and the little potato put out his hand and clasped at it. Lacey saw Col take a shuddering breath. His eyes started to shine in the same way Rex's were. It seemed to be a catching condition. All five of her men gathered around, looking down at the baby they had made. It didn't matter who the little spud's biological father was. What mattered was that he had five fathers ready to love him for the rest of his life, and a mother who loved him more than life itself.

THE END

Made in the USA
Columbia, SC
29 April 2024